THE l

THE PERFECT WEEKEND

JOANNE RYAN

Tamarillas Press

Cover Design: © Joanne Ryan
ISBN: 978-1-913807-22-1

Other books by Joanne Ryan:

Without Reason
All The Lost Years
Not Your Average Girl
The Lodger
The Double
One Night
Lie To Me
The New Neighbours
Keep Your Friends Close
Don't Let Her In
Alone in The Dark
The Sister in Law
The Party
One Click Away

Writing as Marina Johnson:

Fat Girl Slim
Fat Girl Slim Returns
Fat Girl Slim Three
Fat Girl Slim Forever
A Confusion of Murders
So Talk To Me
The Herb Sisters
Say Hello & Wave Goodbye
The Harriet Way

CHAPTER ONE

'I thought we said no presents?'

'It's for both of us, so that doesn't count, does it?' Joe grins, clearly pleased with himself.

'O-k-a-y,' I say, drawing the word out. 'But it's still cheating. And you're the one who made the no presents rule, remember?'

Not entirely true; it was Joe's idea, but we both agreed to it. Despite this being only our first wedding anniversary, we don't want to buy each other pointless gifts just because tradition dictates that we should. We'd rather be spontaneous, surprising each other with 'just because' gifts when the moment feels right.

'It's not useless tat,' Joe says. 'And it's not something you'd secretly hate. It's a present for both of us and I would have done it, anyway. It just happens to coincide with our anniversary. A special offer just dropped into my inbox, so how could I refuse it? It was clearly meant to be, wasn't it?'

'I'm intrigued now. What is it?'

'Two nights at a luxury countryside hotel, complete with a Michelin starred restaurant and a health spa. You know I've got a few days off work next week so there'll be no need to rush to get back on Monday. We can take our time. Have a leisurely breakfast and stop at a country pub for lunch on the way home.'

Joe looks so excited that I try not to let my hesitation show. Normally, I would love a weekend away but having just transitioned from a plaster cast to a walking boot with a three-inch heel, hobbling around the countryside doesn't sound as great to me as it does to him. But I can't let him know that because it would seem really ungrateful.

It is ungrateful.

'You hate the idea, don't you?' Joe frowns.

'No! Of course I don't, it sounds perfect but I'm just worried that it'll be a bit wasted on me. I mean, I can't go on long country walks with this, can I?' I gesture at the Velcro and webbing boot strapped to my lower leg.

'We don't *have* to go on long walks. But you can put weight on it now, and you couldn't before, could you? And you'll soon get rid of the crutches once you're used to it. It'll be the perfect opportunity to ease yourself in with an amble in the countryside. The doctor said you needed to walk on it and not sit around.'

'True,' I admit. 'Short walks will be good.' But I'm the one wearing the boot, not Joe, so he has no idea what it's like. The plaster only came off two days ago, and I was shocked at how painful it was to put weight on my foot after six weeks of hopping around. Like most people who've never broken a bone, Joe doesn't understand what it's like having a broken limb. I didn't either until I broke my ankle and fibula six weeks ago. Two bones at once, because of course, I don't do things by halves.

And it wasn't even the result of some dramatic accident. I simply stepped off a high kerb while on holiday in Spain, twisted my ankle and fell heavily. There was no need for an x-ray to confirm I'd broken my leg because I felt it snap, although learning I'd also broken my ankle was a surprise I could have done without.

Once my leg and ankle were plastered, the extent of my incapacity was a shock, both for me and for Joe. Crutches; dead easy, I assumed. Being fit and healthy, I was confident that I'd get the hang of them in no time, and Joe certainly made it look easy as he bounced around on them with ease. But using crutches with a broken limb is an entirely different experience. There's a constant fear of falling and making things worse. And unlike someone with two functioning legs, I couldn't just put my foot down if I lost my balance. That wasn't an option.

'Besides,' Joe says, reaching across the table to

take my hand. 'We don't have to walk much if you don't want to. We can cosy up in luxury and you can have as much rest as you need. Lie in bed all day if we like. And according to the reviews, the food is to die for.'

'Where is this place?'

'Not telling, because it'll spoil the surprise. All you need to know is that it's deep in the Cotswolds and ultra exclusive, so pack your best stuff. It'll give you a chance to wear one of those sexy little dresses you've got hidden away.'

'With this?' I wave a hand at my strapped-up leg.

Joe doesn't answer right away. Instead, he grabs his plate, strides to the dishwasher, yanks the door open, and hurls it inside with a loud clatter. Then he slams it shut and turns to face me.

'Okay. I'll cancel it. Forget it. Forget I even tried to do something nice. We'll stay here instead. Get a takeaway or maybe just forget it's our first wedding anniversary entirely. Watch telly like a couple of old people.'

'Don't be like that.'

'Like what?' he snaps. 'I try to do something nice and you throw it back in my face.'

'I'm just being realistic. A sexy little dress doesn't exactly go with a giant, clunky walking boot.'

Joe rolls his eyes and makes a tutting sound.

'It's not that though, is it?' he says. 'Not really. This is because you blame me, don't you? For that.' He points at my leg.

'Of course I don't blame you.'

'Yes, you do. I can tell. I committed the crime of making you go on holiday to Spain when you didn't want to. You broke your leg, and it's all my fault.'

'You're being ridiculous. You didn't make it happen.' The words leave my mouth, but I'm not sure I fully believe them. It's irrational, I know, but if we hadn't gone to Spain, I wouldn't have fallen. Or maybe I would; maybe it was my destiny to break my leg no matter where I was. I'll never know. But I know that dealing with it in an English hospital would have been a lot easier than in a Spanish one.

'*Most* people would love having a father with a luxury villa in Marbella, a place they could visit anytime they wanted. *Most* people wouldn't need convincing to go somewhere hot and sunny.' Joe's glare sharpens. '*Most* people would be grateful.'

I can tell by his expression that we're on the verge of a full-blown argument. That's the last thing I want. The thought of us barely speaking for days, circling each other in tense silence, is not how I want to start our second year of marriage. I also don't want to get into another conversation about my dad and his money.

Joe's right about one thing; I *didn't* want to go to Spain, and I felt pressured into it. To me, the house in Marbella is just a place I spent part of my childhood; it doesn't feel like a holiday. But saying that out loud makes me sound spoiled and entitled

– two things I try my hardest *not* to be.

'Look Joe, I am grateful, honestly, and a weekend away is a lovely idea. It's just this leg gets me down, you know? It feels never-ending, like I've been hopping around forever.'

'But you're nearly fixed now, aren't you? Four more weeks in the boot and you'll be back to normal. That's what the consultant said.'

He did say that. But he also said a lot of other things that Joe conveniently didn't hear; things about taking it slow, not pushing myself, or risking setbacks. He warned me that walking would be painful at first, that my calf muscles had wasted away, that I'd need powerful painkillers just to bear weight on it for the first week. I bite down on my irritation. Why does Joe make me feel as if I'm making a meal of everything?

Maybe I am.

'I am on the mend,' I say. 'And I *do* want to go away this weekend and I don't blame you for what happened in Spain. If I'd been paying attention and not wearing those ridiculous wedge sandals, it wouldn't have happened. It's my fault, not yours.'

'I can cancel it if you really don't want to go.' Joe sits down across from me, a small smile playing at his lips. 'I don't mind.'

Yes, you do, and I'm not playing this game; me pretending I want to go while you pretend you'd cancel without resentment.

'No, we're going.' I stand up, wincing as pain shoots through my leg. Grabbing hold of the crutches that are leaning against the table, I loop my arms over them. 'I'm going upstairs to pack.'

'Are you sure? I mean it, I can cancel.'

'No. I *want* to go. It'll be a change of scenery. You'd better pack, too, unless you're planning on wearing the same clothes for the next three days.'

'Already done.'

'What?'

'All packed. I would have packed for you too, but I know how fussy you are about what you wear and that you'll want to take half your wardrobe. Impressed?' he asks with a grin. 'Just proves that I can plan a surprise for you without you knowing because you didn't have a clue, did you?'

'No, I didn't. I am impressed. I thought you were lying in bed when, clearly, you weren't.' And you had no intention of cancelling, either, did you?

'If you want, you could just tell me what you want to take and I'll come up and pack it for you,' Joe offers.

'No, it's okay. I need to move and get walking on this leg. I'll call you when I'm done.'

Going out into the hallway, with the help of the crutches, I clomp my way slowly up the stairs and into our bedroom. An open suitcase lies on our bed with Joe's clothes already inside, looking as if they've been flung there from a distance. I walk over to the bed and smile to myself as I take them out, refold them and put them back in. Joe is so loveable and thoughtful and I feel bad that he's gone to the trouble of organising a surprise and

I've nearly spoilt it all by being miserable. What does it matter than I have a clumpy walking boot? It doesn't. Not at all. Okay, he always seems to get his way, but does it really matter? It's not worth falling out over a weekend away because all he's trying to do is make me happy.

By the time I've selected two 'sexy dresses' as Joe calls them; a black knee length silky sheath and a frothy cream strappy cocktail dress plus two pairs of trousers, jumpers and underwear, my leg is aching, so I sit down on the bed as I put everything into the case. I also put in a pair of black heels to go with the dresses, plus an extra pair of trainers besides the boots I'm wearing. Despite only being able to wear one of each shoe, I put both in the case because it seems weird just taking one. Joe says there's a spa at the hotel, so maybe I'll get a manicure and a pedicure. My toes have been woefully neglected these past weeks and a spot of bright colour on them will make me feel better.

Stop being miserable, Beth, and enjoy the lovely surprise your husband has arranged for you.

◆ ◆ ◆

'It's snowing.' I look out of the car window at the flurries of snow whirling around.

'Great, isn't it?' Joe grins, glancing at me. 'It'll be so pretty. We can sit inside all cosy next to a roaring fire while we sip hot chocolate laced with rum.'

'Sounds perfect.' I turn the heated seat up a notch, swallowing down my question as to whether it was wise to drive in this weather. Before we left home, the weather forecasters issued an amber warning, advising the public to only make journeys if they're absolutely necessary. Joe knows this, but I don't want to mention it because he'll think I'm trying to make an excuse not to go and I'm not, now. I'm looking forward to it.

'How much further is it?' I ask. The snow flurries are becoming thicker as they spin around, whirlpool like, before hitting the windscreen.

'Not telling you, it's a secret. You'll just have to wait and see.'

'Are you sure you know the way? I could put the sat nav on, just to make sure we're going the right way.'

'Don't you dare touch it.' He laughs. 'You're just trying to find out where the hotel is, but I know the way, so you don't need to worry. They emailed me with directions and we'll be there before it gets dark. Maybe we'll get snowed in for a few weeks and I won't be able to go to work.'

If Joe is confident we'll arrive before dark, then the hotel can't be far away. It's only just past three o'clock, but the sky is so heavy with snow it's already dimming the light. In hindsight, we should have left earlier and skipped our leisurely lunch. What was meant to be a quick sandwich stop at a charming country pub turned into a two-hour break, thanks to slow service and an irresistibly cosy log fire. I also had two large glasses of wine, which has made me decidedly sleepy.

Joe's booked us a table at the Michelin starred restaurant for tonight – apparently the hotel has several excellent restaurants – and he's been teasing me with snippets from the menu. Leaning back in my seat, I close my eyes and try to guess where we're going. We've been driving for about an hour and while the road signs were familiar at first, we're now passing signs to places I've never heard of. The wide A roads have turned into winding country lanes, barely wide enough for one car. Despite it being a Saturday, the roads are eerily empty. Most people have heeded the forecast and chosen to stay home.

'Shit.'

Joe's voice startles me, and I jolt, opening my eyes. The two glasses of wine did their job and I must have dozed off. It's completely dark now, and through the windscreen, I can barely see a thing. Snow is coming down thick and fast. A quick glance at the dashboard tells me it's almost four o'clock. How long was I asleep?

'What's wrong?'

Joe doesn't answer, but hunches over the steering wheel, eyes fixed on the dashboard.

'Joe?'

'There's a warning light on.'

'For what?'

'I don't know.'

I lean towards him, squinting at the screen.

'Where? I can't see it.'

'It just went off. No, wait, it's back. And now it's gone again.'

'Probably just a faulty sensor or something,' I say.

'No, I don't think so. The car's not driving right and that light's been flickering on and off for the last ten miles.'

'But this car isn't even old.'

'Tell me about it.'

'How hasn't it been driving right?'

Before he can answer, the car shudders violently and rolls to a stop. Joe switches off the ignition, and instantly, we're plunged into total darkness.

'Why are we stopping?'

'We don't have a lot of choice. There's something wrong with the car.'

'But we're in the middle of nowhere!'

'I can't drive a broken car, Beth.'

'We could go really slowly?'

'That's what I've been doing for the last half an hour. It keeps juddering and jumping around. Who knows what damage I'll do to the engine if we keep going.'

'Oh.' Outside, the only shapes visible are the faint outlines of trees flanking the narrow road. There aren't any streetlights. No signs of life. Just endless darkness and falling snow. 'We'll have to call the AA or whoever it is we're with.' I root through my handbag and pull out my phone. I know I have the number saved somewhere, though

I've never had to use it before. As the screen lights up, there are no bars at the top. I have no signal.

'Have you got a signal, Joe?'

'Nope. Nothing. Not even one bar.'

I shove my phone back into my bag and zip it up.

'How far is it to the hotel?' I ask. 'We must be close because you said it wasn't far just before I fell asleep.'

Silence.

'Joe?'

'Yeah, well, the thing is, I think we're lost.'

CHAPTER TWO

'Lost? How can we be lost?'

'I couldn't see the road signs properly because of the snow. It's not my fault there's practically a blizzard out there.'

No, but it *is* your fault we ignored the warnings about non-essential travel. I don't say it, though, because what's done is done, and blaming Joe won't help. Besides, I could have spoken up earlier, couldn't I?

'What was the last sign you saw? We must be near somewhere, a village or something, so we could walk there. Nowhere is very far away in this country.'

Joe doesn't answer. When I glance at him through the dim light, he's staring out of the window, his expression miserable.

'Joe?'

He lets out a heavy sigh. 'I don't know. Like I said, I couldn't see, so I just kept going. I know we're in some forest – can't remember the name –

but I thought if I kept going in a straight line, we'd hit a village eventually.'

'So you don't actually know where we are?' I wince at the way the words come out. Much sharper than I intended.

'Not really.'

'Great. Then we'll just have to walk and hope the next village isn't too far away.'

'You can't, though, can you?' Joe says. 'Not with your broken leg. It's too dangerous. You could slip over.'

That's when I look out of the window and see the snow piling up on the road, getting deeper by the minute. It's coming down thick and fast now, big, heavy flakes swirling around us.

'We don't have a lot of choice, do we?' I say. 'I don't think there'll be any cars coming along this road to help us because sensible people won't be coming out in this weather, will they? And we can't stay in the car because we'll freeze to death with no heating. We don't even have a blanket, let alone any food or water.'

'Plenty of water around to drink,' Joe quips. 'We just have to melt it.'

I should laugh to lighten the moment, but I can't make myself because it's not funny, Joe, not funny at all. I'm majorly pissed off.

'I'll go,' he says. 'It'll be quicker on my own. I'll keep walking until I find someone, then come back and get you.'

'No thanks. I don't fancy staying here on my

own. We're in the middle of nowhere and it's pitch-black outside. There could be an axe murderer lurking out there for all we know.'

It's cold, too. Bloody cold. The heated seat has gone off, as has the car heater, and the cold is already penetrating my body. Fumbling in my jacket pocket for my gloves, I realise I didn't bring them. The jacket I'm wearing isn't much help either; it's lightly quilted and suitable for wearing in the warmth of the car but not much else. Even if I could walk, I'm hardly dressed for this weather; pretty stupid of me, considering it's the end of January. I should have been better prepared because this jacket isn't any good for country walks, either. Or maybe I never intended going on any because it's a good excuse if you don't have a coat to wear, isn't it?

'I'll be as quick as I can and you can lock the doors while I'm gone,' Joe says.

'Try starting the car again. Now it's had a rest for a while, it might be okay.'

'It won't.'

'You don't know that,' I say, suddenly hopeful. 'Even if it goes just long enough to get us to somewhere inhabited.'

Sighing, Joe fumbles around in the darkness and presses the ignition button.

Silence.

'You've got your foot on the brake, haven't you?' I ask.

'I know how to start the car,' he snaps. 'I'm not

stupid. The engine is dead. This car's not going anywhere.'

'It's only a couple of years old!'

'I know, but how old it is doesn't matter, does it? It's not working and we need to decide what to do because this snow is getting heavier and the longer we sit here, the worse it gets.'

I sigh. How can we have come out so unprepared for this? People die of the cold, don't they?

'If I walk up the road a bit, I might get a mobile signal,' Joe says.

'Do you think?'

'Yeah, it's worth a try, isn't it? This bit here could be a dead spot and a hundred yards could make a big difference. Once I've got a signal, I can call someone for help. If the hotel is nearby, they might even send someone out to get us.'

'But you don't know where we are.'

'I can look at Google maps if I have a signal.'

A hundred yards. How far away is that? Could I walk that far with Joe? I never could do distances, a hundred yards or ten, it's all the same to me.

'I could come with you,' I say.

'No. You stay here. There's no point in us both getting soaked. I don't want you falling over, either.'

'Okay. But don't go too far, will you? Come back if there's no signal, don't keep on walking because you might get lost.'

'I won't get lost,' he snaps. 'All I have to do is follow the road.' I bite my tongue to stop myself from reminding him that's how he got us lost in the first place. He opens the door, letting in a blast of icy air and snow.

'Be careful,' I say as he clambers out.

'I'll be fine. Lock the doors if you feel nervous.' With that, he slams the door and trudges off up the road, lighting the way with his phone torch. The snow is coming down so heavily that he soon disappears from sight and even squinting and thrusting my face close to the windscreen, I can no longer see him or the light from his phone. Wrapping my arms around my body to warm myself up, I silently will him to hurry up and come back.

What if he falls over and hurts himself? What if he can't get up again?

Stop catastrophising.

But I can't help it; we've been unbelievably stupid and the darkness around the car is oppressive, the swirling snow making me feel as if I'm in some sort of nightmarish kaleidoscope. *Please hurry up, Joe, please.*

It seems as if he's been gone for ages, but it's my mind is playing tricks on me because there is no music or anything to distract me. I note the time on my phone; four-thirty-five. It'll be slow going in the snow and he's only wearing shoes, not boots, which will make it harder. Although I can't see him, it's so dark out there that he could be quite close and I wouldn't see him, anyway. Even his phone torch seemed a weak light in all that darkness.

I wouldn't see anyone.

Someone could be out there watching me and I wouldn't know.

Stop, Beth, stop. No one is out there because, unlike you and Joe, nobody else is stupid enough to go out on a day like this. Joe will be back any minute, so all I have to do is lock the doors and wait. We'll laugh about this when we've been rescued and are cosy and warm tonight.

I check my watch; four-forty-two.

Yep, any minute now he'll be back and help will be on its way.

◆ ◆ ◆

Five-fifty-seven.

Face it, Beth, he's not coming back.

What am I going to do and where the hell is he? He's been gone for over an hour. He was only going to walk to get a signal; did he keep going to get help, not telling me because he knew I'd make a big fuss about him leaving me here?

No. Something's happened to him; he's fallen and hurt himself and is lying in the road with a layer of snow covering him.

The thought is unbearable.

I have to go out and search for him. If I stick to the road, I shouldn't get lost. My broken leg isn't properly protected, wrapped in padding and straps and I can barely feel my toes they're so frozen so getting them wet won't make much difference. Twisting in my seat, I grab my crutches from the back seat and pull them through to the front, propping them in the footwell.

Move.

My brain is telling me to get going, because delaying won't achieve anything, but a tiny part of me still hopes that Joe will suddenly appear, complete with breakdown truck.

I have a horrible feeling that something terrible has happened to him.

Get out there, Beth, and find him before it's too late. As I reach for the door handle, I suddenly sense that I'm not alone. Peering through the swirling snow on the windscreen, I see nothing. The snow is beginning to cover the glass and soon I'll be sealed in here, like a tomb. Twisting around to look through the back window, I see it's the same. Even if someone were there, I wouldn't be able to see them. Should I get out or sit here, like an idiot?

Get out.

Thud.

Something, or someone, slams heavily against the passenger side door, making me recoil back in my seat, heart racing. Staring at the handle, I watch it shake as whatever it is hits it again. Throwing myself to one side, I lie across the driver's seat, and stay low. Seconds later, the driver's door shudders as something bashes against that side, too.

Something heavy.

Has a vehicle skidded into me? My scrambled thoughts try to make sense of it, logically I know there are no lights or sounds of a car because I would have seen both, despite the poor visibility. Besides, if it were a vehicle, it would have most likely crushed both the car and me. Both sides of the car thud simultaneously, over and over again, and I cover my head with my arms, close my eyes, and wish it away.

And then, as suddenly as it began, it stops.

Maybe they, whatever they were, have gone.

Pulling myself upright, my heart slows, but my mind races. Could it be wild animals that have lost their bearings in the snow? Deer or wild boar, perhaps. There must be at least two of them to be on each side of the car at the same time.

Yes. That must be it. Nothing to fear. They've already run off into the night, more frightened of me than I am of them.

So get out of the car.

I stretch my hand towards the door handle but freeze when I hear a peculiar, low, unnatural noise that has no place inside this car. At the same moment that the cogs in my brain finally whir into action and acknowledge that it's the sound of an animal, the passenger door window comes into focus and I see a huge beast staring back at me, its lips drawn back in a snarl, its snout pressed up against the window, its breath fogging the glass. A strangled gasp escapes me as I whip my head toward the driver's side, just in time to see its twin clawing frantically at the door. Huge paws scrape against the glass, screeching, like nails on a blackboard.

Not deer. Not wild boars.

Two enormous dogs.

And they're trying to get in.

Frozen with terror, I sink back across the seat, hands clamping over my head. It's fine. The doors are locked. Whatever is outside may be huge and ferocious, but they're not capable of opening a car door. If I stay perfectly still, they'll go away. They went away once so they'll go again, so long as I stay quiet.

Where the hell have they come from?

Clamping my hands tightly over my ears to block out the snarls and yelps doesn't work because I can still hear them. Or perhaps it's in my head. They'll leave soon, they will. After a while, their paws stop beating on the car and the eerie silence that I hate so much is back again.

They've gone.

My pounding heartbeat slowly returns to normal, and my breath is no longer coming in ragged gasps. Now what? Do I go outside and search for Joe? What if the dogs are still out there, waiting?

Oh God. What if they've found Joe first?

I open my eyes and stare into the blackness beyond the windscreen. The snow is still falling heavily, swirling in chaotic patterns. Who knew it could snow this much here? My vision adjusts to the spinning flakes and I see it.

A face.

Pressed against the glass.

A scarf covers the lower half, a hood shrouding the rest, leaving only two eyes staring straight at me.

For a fleeting second, hope flares in my chest. Help. At last.

But before I can move, he's gone.

A second later, the dogs return, leaping against the car, their snarls filling the air. And then the face is back – this time at the passenger window, hands cupped around his eyes as he peers inside.

Maybe he can't see me. It's dark in here, and I'm lying down. In an agony of indecision, I don't know whether to make myself known. He could be here to help me.

So why is he making no attempt to control those dogs?

The driver's side door handle rattles. He's pulling at it, yanking harder and harder when it refuses to open. The snarls outside grow more frenzied, the dogs leaping and scratching at the car. A thumping noise joins the vicious snarls of the dogs as the man pounds his fist against the window, each blow harder, louder.

He's not here to help me.

He's here to attack me.

Panic surges through me. Even if I scramble out of the driver's side door, he'd be upon me before I could get more than a few steps away.

That's if the dogs didn't get to me first.

The pounding stops and I pull myself upright, scanning the darkness, but I can see nothing.

Has he gone?

And then he's at the passenger window, face pressed against the glass, pulling at the handle. The pounding resumes, harder than before. He's shouting, but the words are hard to hear over the sound of my heartbeat and the dogs barking. The dogs growl wildly beside him, their excitement mounting. I realise there's nothing I can do; I'm trapped.

There's no way out.

So I do the only thing possible.

I open my mouth and scream.

CHAPTER THREE

He's gone.

Astonishingly, when I started screaming, he disappeared, taking the dogs with him. Is this some kind of trick? A ploy to lure me out of the car so he can ambush me?

I don't know.

Now it's unnervingly quiet, amplifying the suffocating sense of isolation. It feels as though I'm trapped in a box, completely cut off from the world. Desperate to do something, I grab my crutches and place a hand on the door handle. Am I really about to get out? Possibly. Probably. My only alternative is to sit here and freeze to death.

Thud.

Oh God. He's back.

The pounding starts again, accompanied by muffled shouting, but this time, the dogs are nowhere to be seen or heard. I squeeze my eyes shut, reminding myself that he can't get in. I'm safe. Sort of. Unless he smashes the window.

Bang, bang, bang.

Beth. Open the door.

My eyes snap open. He said my name. How is that possible?

Steeling myself, I turn my head and focus on the figure hammering on the glass. There is no scarf covering his face this time, no hood.

It's Joe.

Relief surges through me at the sight of him. With shaking fingers, after several attempts, I flick the handle to unlock the door and Joe pulls it open with difficulty, struggling against the snowdrift, because somehow, the snow is so deep it's piled above the car door.

'Thank God you're okay!' I gasp, bursting into tears. 'I thought you were dead.' I clutch hold of his hands and cling onto them tightly.

'Of course I'm okay. Why were you screaming?' His tone is sharp, almost irritated, as if I've done something wrong.

'You were gone so long,' I gabble, my words running into each other. 'A man was here with enormous dogs trying to break into the car. Didn't you see them? Get in! Quick! We need to lock the doors because he could be back any minute. Here, I'll move over to the driver's seat and you can sit in mine.' I try to pull him inside, but he twists his fingers out of my grasp.

'It's fine. Come on, swing your legs around and get out.' He steps back to make way for me and I stare at him in confusion. He needs to get in this car and lock the doors. It's not safe out there. Why isn't he listening to me? I open my mouth to tell him, but before I can speak, the bulky figure of a man appears, looming behind him.

'Joe! Look out!' I scream. 'Behind you!'

'Stop screaming,' Joe snaps. 'Calm down. You're being hysterical. It's just Mick, for God's sake. He's trying to help us.'

'Help?'

'Yes. He has a truck and is going to take us to his place. He was trying to help you out of the car when you started screaming the place down. Mick came to get you because he's dressed for this and I'm not.' He reaches for my hand. 'Come on, swing your legs around and I'll help you stand. The crutches won't work. The snow's too deep.'

He turns his head, murmuring something to Mick. Then he laughs.

A flush of embarrassment creeps over me. My panic feels misplaced now, maybe even ridiculous. Joe turns back, pulling me toward him.

'How was I supposed to know he was trying to help?' I murmur as he pulls me to my feet. 'Those dogs scared me to death and when he started banging on the window, I panicked. I thought he was going to attack me. You were gone so long I thought something bad had happened to you.'

He sighs but doesn't answer, so I shut up, because I'm clearly making this worse. Once I'm upright, Joe puts his arms underneath me and picks me up to carry me.

'I can walk. If you support me, I can manage,' I insist.

'For Christ's sake, just do what I ask,' he mutters.

He trudges forward, sinking deep into the snow with each step. The snow is deep and now reaches halfway up his legs. His irritation silences me, and I focus on peering through the swirling blizzard, trying to make out where we're headed. The only sound is Joe's laboured breathing, his pace slowing with every step.

I want to ask where Mick went, and more importantly, where the dogs are, but I bite my tongue. I'm safe. Joe's safe. That's all that matters.

Then, out of the darkness, a massive vehicle looms in front of us. The towering wheels make us seem insignificant in comparison. For a split second, panic grips me – I'm certain it's going to plough straight into us – but then I realise the headlights are on and the engine is running. The truck is motionless. Parked.

Maybe I do overreact. Perhaps Joe's right.

When we reach the passenger side of the truck, we come to a halt.

'We'll have to wait for Mick. I'm not going to be able to lift you up there on my own.'

The door is high, the bottom of it almost shoulder height to Joe. I can't imagine anyone being strong enough to lift me up there and there's no way I'll be able to climb up on one good leg.

'Will you be alright to stand for a few minutes?' Joe asks. 'I don't think I can carry you any longer.'

'Of course I will.'

He lowers me carefully, and for the first time in hours, I stand properly. The cold is instant and brutal, biting through the thin layers of my walking boot and sock, sending a sharp shock through my foot. I dig my good foot into the snow and cling to Joe for balance, shivering violently.

Then, without warning, Joe leans in and whispers urgently in my ear.

'Stay still. Don't move.'

'What…?'

'And for fuck's sake, don't scream.'

A deep, guttural growl rumbles from behind me.

My breath catches as I slowly turn my head. Two massive hounds stand at the front of the truck, their teeth bared in silent snarls. Their eyes glint in the dim light, muscles tensed. They move closer to us, their snouts drawn showing huge, sharp teeth. One lets out a shrill bark while the other continues to growl menacingly.

I tighten my grip on Joe, and though he says nothing, I can feel his tension, his fear.

'Abel! Cain! Here!' The man's voice is loud, deep and commanding. The dogs freeze for a moment before pivoting and racing off into the darkness. Seconds later, the hooded figure of the man I now know as Mick lumbers past us to the back of the truck, the dogs bounding along behind him. Our overnight bag is tucked under one of his arms, my crutches underneath the other. There's the sound of a truck door being opened and the scrabble of paws as the dogs' clamber in. This is followed by a thud – I guess of our belongings being thrown in, and the sound of the door as it's slammed shut.

And then Mick is in front of us, a giant of a man, towering over Joe, who's six feet tall but suddenly seems small in comparison. I'm not short, yet next to him, I feel tiny. He reaches up and pulls down his scarf, revealing a thick, black beard.

'Mick,' Joe says. 'Beth didn't realise you were trying to help. She got a bit nervous on her own, what with it being dark and everything.'

Anger sparks in me; he's apologising for me. If there's any apologising to be done, I'll do it myself, thank you. Although have I actually got anything to say sorry for? Joe abandons me for over an hour and then mad dogs and a giant appear out of nowhere. Is it any wonder I thought I was being attacked? How was I supposed to know he was trying to help?

I'm not a mind reader.

Mick doesn't reply. Instead, he pulls open the truck door, turns to me, and without a word, lifts me effortlessly into his arms. As if I weigh nothing, he climbs the steps and, in a single, fluid motion, plonks me down on the seat.

Then, just as quickly, he jumps back down and strides around the front of the truck. Joe clambers up into the cab, and I shuffle over to make room for him. We both buckle our seatbelts, and as I settle in, I look at Joe properly for the first time in the dim light. His face is pale, drawn with exhaustion. His thin jacket is soaked through, his hair dripping. When his hand brushes mine as he fastens his seatbelt, the icy touch sends a jolt through me – he's so cold. Guilt washes over me. I'd been so wrapped up in my own fear and misery that I hadn't considered what he's been through. He's been out in the freezing cold for ages and all I've done is feel sorry for myself. Taking hold of his frozen fingers in mine, I hold them between my hands. My hands are cold, too, but nowhere near as icy as his. He turns to me in surprise, giving me a small smile.

'Alright. Let's go,' Mick says as he climbs into the cab beside me and slams the door shut. Without waiting for a response, he pushes the gear stick into gear, and with the engine rumbling beneath us, we lurch forward, making our way through the forest.

◆ ◆ ◆

'Beth.' Joe whispers, shaking my arm. 'Beth.'

My eyes fly open. How on earth did I fall asleep? Just seconds ago we were driving through the forest and my mind was racing with questions – where we were, how long Joe had to walk for, if he was okay. A thousand things I wanted to know that the presence of Mick stopped me from asking.

'I must have dozed off.'

'It's the warmth. I feel sleepy too.'

The cab is toasty; my hands are no longer icy

and when I breathe, clouds of vapour don't billow from my mouth. Blinking away my drowsiness, I look through the windscreen to see that we've pulled up in front of an enormous house. No, not a house, a mansion. It's huge and looms before us, vast and imposing. Confused, I look around the surroundings to see that there are no other houses in sight, just trees, nothing but trees. I assumed we were heading towards a town. Mick is no longer next to me in the driving seat and I wonder how long we've been here.

Where are we?' I ask Joe.

Before he can answer, the passenger door is yanked open from the outside, and within seconds, Joe climbs down. Mick hauls himself into the cab, and I instinctively shift toward the edge of the seat.

'Okay?' White teeth flash at me and then I'm lifted and taken out of the cab. I expect to be put down right away, but he carries me around the truck and up the stone steps to a grand set of double doors. Only then does he lower me onto my feet before striding off without another word. I steady myself against the wall, hesitant to move without my crutches, as I watch Joe climb the steps toward me.

'Okay?' he asks, as he stands next to me.

'Yeah, all good. Where are we?'

'Mick's house. The weather's too bad to take us into town tonight, so we'll have to stay here.' He leans in slightly and lowers his voice. 'This is like a stately home. Do you think Mick is a lord or something?'

'Maybe, judging by the size of the place. Where's he gone?'

The barking of the dogs answers my question. Joe and I exchange a worried look. Are they coming into the house? I don't relish the thought of being anywhere near those monster dogs.

Joe and I turn to look as we hear the sound of the front door being opened. A tall, thin man is standing in the doorway. He smiles and beckons us inside. 'Please, come in, you must be freezing. Come through and warm up. Evan,' he says, thrusting a hand out towards me. 'Pleased to meet you.'

'Beth,' I say, shaking his hand whilst clutching onto the wall.

He shakes Joe's hand and then turns and strides across a vast hallway towards a doorway. Grabbing hold of Joe's arm, we follow behind, leaving a trail of water on the pristine tiles in our wake. The doorway leads into a large lounge where we're greeted by a roaring, open fire and a clutter of heavy old furniture that's traditional and solid; exactly what you'd expect in a country manor. Nothing minimalistic here; the room is warm and cosy and despite being so big and filled with several large sofas, big armchairs, enormous bookcases and a sideboard, it doesn't feel crowded at all.

'Please. Sit.' Crossing to the fireplace, where he

picks up an ancient-looking poker, Evan prods the coals of the fire, sending embers shooting up the chimney. I unzip my coat and pull it off, wondering where I can put it. It's sopping wet, as are my trousers, and by the feel of it, my underwear, too. Joe does the same and while I'm looking for a suitable place to put them, Evan walks over, takes the coats from us and casually throws them onto an armchair. We settle ourselves onto a large sofa facing the fire and I revel in the warmth whilst wondering how much of a damp patch I'm going to leave behind when I get up. We're still wearing our wet and squishy shoes, but it feels awkward to take them off. Evan crosses to the doorway and goes out and a few moments later, he's back.

'Mick will bring in your crutches and put your belongings in your room once he's seen to the dogs. Maria is rustling up some supper, but it'll take a while. Give you both time to get some dry clothes on.'

I give Joe a questioning look while Evan's back is turned and he shrugs. Like me, he assumed this was Mick's house, but maybe it's not.

Maybe he's staff.

Evan is well spoken; not quite received pronunciation, but not far off.

'Rotten bad luck, breaking down like that.' Evan flashes a brief smile. 'With a bit of luck it'll all have thawed by tomorrow or if not, the snow ploughs will be out to scoop it all up and we can get you towed to a garage. The snow's too heavy to risk taking you anywhere tonight. Mick says you got lost, Joe, is that right?'

'Sadly, yes.' Joe looks embarrassed.

'Easily done.' Evan sits back, stretches his legs out and steeples his fingers together. 'Maria will make up a room for you.' He's thin; spare, I suppose, is the right word. Older than Joe and me, I think, but not by much. Late thirties, possibly.

'Thank you, that's very kind.'

He waves my thanks away and we sit in silence, the ticking of the ancient clock on the ornate mantelpiece the only sound.

'Maria will be along to show you to your room soon, but in the meantime, how about a drink, something to warm you up, eh?'

He jumps up from the chair, crosses to a huge sideboard and takes three glasses out of the cupboard. His movements are swift, as is his walk, everything done quickly and with the minimum of wasted effort.

'Whisky?' he offers. Without waiting for an answer, he uncaps a bottle and pours three large measures, cups all the glasses together in his long, thin fingers and carries them over to us. I take one but have no intention of drinking it; I can't bear the smell of whisky, let alone the taste.

Evan sits back down in the armchair and raises his glass.

'To the good old British weather.'

For politeness' sake, I put the glass to my lips and pretend to take a sip. Joe swallows half his glass in one go. When Evan isn't looking, I'll give him mine.

'Where were you headed to?' Evan asks.

I look at Joe because I can't answer that and I'll be interested to know, too.

'The Swanhope. A hotel out Fledgely Way.'

'Very nice.' Evan nods. 'Been there a few times myself. Not to stay, you understand, but for the restaurant. They have an excellent chef there.'

Now I know I'm none the wiser because I've never heard of it. Will we still go there tomorrow if the weather permits, or just go straight home? As Joe's car is going to need repairing, maybe we should skip the hotel and go home.

'You're a long way off, though,' he adds. 'It's a good thirty plus miles from here.'

Joe doesn't respond, but tips the rest of his whisky into his mouth. I nudge my glass against his and he takes it from me.

'So Joe, what's your business? I mean, what do you do?'

'Accountant.' Joe laughs. 'Not very exciting, I'm afraid.'

'Nothing wrong with being an accountant. Where would we be without accountants, eh? In a right old mess, that's where. And what about you, Beth? What do you do?'

'Nothing at the moment,' I say. 'I'm between jobs, plus, I'm waiting for this to mend.' I wave a hand at my leg.

'Yes. Of course. These things take time. Broken

leg or ankle?'

'Both,' I say with a laugh.

'Nasty.'

'Yes.' I don't elaborate, unwilling to relate the story of a pair of wedge sandals and a high kerb. I've heard enough jokes about taking more water with it to last me a lifetime. Evan studies me for a moment. Was my answer rude? Possibly. But it's too late now.

'You know.' Evan holds his glass up in my direction. 'You look familiar to me. Have we met?'

'No.' I shake my head and smile. 'We haven't.'

'Hmm.' He studies me. 'Are you an actress? You look so familiar. I'm sure I've seen your face before. I never forget a face.'

'No,' I smile. 'I'm flattered that you might think I'm an actress, but I'm afraid I'm very ordinary. Very dull.'

Evan tips his head to one side, studying me. 'So you've never been in the public eye?'

'No.' I laugh. 'If only.'

His eyes linger on my face as he sips his whisky and I turn away from his gaze to stare into the flames of the fire, telling myself that it's the heat of the fire making my face hot.

And not the fact that I just lied.

CHAPTER FOUR

'Wow, this is what you call a guestroom,' Joe says as Maria exits the room, closing the door behind her. He looks around. 'Makes me think of Buckingham Palace, all that gilt, dark furniture and swirly carpets.'

'Buckingham Palace?'

'Yeah, seen it on the telly. Old money, chintzy grandeur, with massive rooms that go on forever.'

I limp to the large sofa sitting opposite the huge bed and sit down, laying my crutches on the floor. Walking's much easier now I have them back, although the stairs were a bit of a challenge. I discovered that hopping up the stairs on my good leg was more practical than trying to walk.

'Wonder what's for dinner?' Joe undoes his shirt buttons. 'I'm bloody starving. That pub lunch didn't touch the sides. Do you think we should dress up?'

'Dress up?'

'Yeah, because he's posh, isn't he? He probably puts a suit and tie on. A dinner jacket, maybe.'

'I think you've been watching too much TV.'

Joe laughs, easing the water-stained trousers off his legs and dropping them onto the floor next to his shoes.

'I wonder if he has any more staff or if Moody Maria and Mick are it.'

'Shh.'

'It's okay, she's gone, and if she hasn't, eavesdroppers never hear good about themselves, do they?'

'She wasn't moody.'

'She was. Miserable. Monosyllabic. Probably pissed off that she had to make a bed up and cook us something to eat. Looking after one bloke is a doddle and now she has to do some work catering for us.'

'Yeah, but we're only here for one night. Mick can tow us to a garage tomorrow and we'll be gone.'

He doesn't answer, too busy opening the doors of the immense wardrobe and sticking his head inside.

'Joe?'

'I reckon three people my size could fit inside here easily. Even you'd have trouble filling it with all your clothes.'

'Ha ha.'

'You're not denying you have a lot of clothes?'

'I'm absolutely not,' I say. 'But you have more.'

'Do not.'

This room is vast and Maria referred to it as the 'green room' when she ushered us in. The wallpaper is green foliage with monstrous flowers splattered over a trellis pattern and it clashes horrifically with the carpet, a tiny checked nightmare that could make me throw up if I looked at it too long. Complete with a pile of fresh towels on the bed and an ensuite bathroom, we could be in a very upmarket and old-fashioned hotel.

I pull off my boot, ease my other leg out of my walking boot and peel my damp trousers off, tossing it all next to Joe's clothing on the floor.

'We should dump all that in the bath, otherwise it'll make a right mess of the carpet,' I say. 'I must have left a damp patch on that sofa.'

'You mean *I* should put it all in the bath?' Joe asks, closing the wardrobe door.

I laugh as he scoops it all up and takes it into the bathroom, returning seconds later.

'The breakdown insurance will give us a hire car while ours is getting repaired. Do you think it would be better to go straight home rather than go to the hotel?' I ask. 'If this snow hangs around, it might be safer.'

'Hmm, don't know. Seems a shame to waste it, seeing as it's booked and paid for.'

'They might give you a refund, with it being special circumstances, because no one saw that weather coming.'

'Maybe. Although I doubt it. The Swanhope is

always booked up, and I was lucky to get us a room. I can't see them giving me a refund just because my car broke down.' He rips off the rest of his clothes. 'I'm going to take a shower.' He grins, standing in front of me, hands on hips.

'Stop showing off.'

'What? Can't help it if I'm proud of my working out. I don't look like an accountant, do I?'

'No, you don't, but you never did, anyway.' He didn't. When we met, he was in good shape, but now, after increasing his sessions in the gym, Joe has a body with a six-pack to be proud of.

He struts to the bathroom, turning as he reaches the doorway.

'Want to join me?'

'I'd love to, but for this.' I pull a disappointed face and look at my leg.

'I can hold you up. I'm strong, you know.'

'Yeah, and what if you drop me? It's not your leg that's broken, is it?'

The bathroom door closes with a click, my refusal not even meriting a response.

Lying back on the bed, I decide that hungry as I am, I'm much rather not have to eat dinner and make polite conversation with someone I don't know. This was supposed to be a romantic weekend away for the two of us, not dinner with a complete stranger who's rescued us from a blizzard. I settle back on the pillow for a rest but have barely caught my breath before Joe appears from the bathroom, hair wet, towel wrapped around him.

'I'm done. You'd better get a move on. We don't want to be late.'

Picking up the case from the floor, he flings it onto the end of the bed, opens it and busies himself with rooting through the clothes. Heaving myself off the bed, I don't bother putting the boot back on but hop to the bathroom on crutches. Getting myself into the shower isn't too bad as I've had plenty of practice and am used to showering, flamingo style, on one leg. By the time I get out, the hot water has done its job and I feel re-energised and properly warm again. Thoughtfully, fresh underwear has appeared in the bathroom, curtesy of Joe. I put it on and hop back into the bedroom.

'I thought you could wear this.' He's holding up the black dress.

'Absolutely not.'

'Why not?'

'Because…'

'You can't pitch up in your underwear.'

'It's too much.'

'No, it's not.'

He has a determined look on his face, so, knowing it's pointless to argue over something so trivial as what to wear, I give in. By the time we're ready to go downstairs, I'm wearing black tights, heels, the black dress and a face full of makeup.

'I'm ridiculously overdressed.' I stand in front of Joe.

'You look hot.'

'I don't want to look hot. I think I should change; put my jeans and a jumper on.'

'Now you're being ridiculous. Come on, stop fussing. Let's get downstairs before Moody Maria comes looking for us.' Before I can argue anymore, Joe opens the door and heads out along the landing towards the stairs. I clatter behind on my crutches in my stupid little black dress, walking boot on one leg, heeled black stiletto on the other.

Totally over the top.

Joe stopped short of wearing a tie, but only because he doesn't have one with him, but he looks ultra smart in dark green trousers and a white linen shirt which he hung in the bathroom for the creases to drop out whilst I was having a shower. He says we should treat tonight as if we're at the hotel and make the most of the hospitality on offer.

And that I should stop being so awkward.

'We're going to look so stupid, Joe,' I hiss as I hobble behind him down the stairs.

'Stop moaning,' he says cheerfully.

Maria is waiting in the hall when we get to the bottom of the stairs and, with a nod to us, walks briskly to a door opposite the lounge. We follow her into a vast room, this one furnished with a formal dining table that would easily seat twelve but has places set for only three. Evan is seated at one end of the table and whilst he's not wearing a tie, he has changed his clothes. He stands up to greet us, insisting we sit on either side of him. His eyes sweep up and down my body as I settle into my seat and lean my crutches on the chair next to me.

'So nice to see that you've both made the effort,' Evan says once we're seated. 'May I say, Beth, you look absolutely enchanting this evening?'

'Thank you.' I silently curse Joe.

'So many people don't bother nowadays, do they? Preferring to slob around as if they're taking a trip to McDonalds.'

Joe flashes me an 'I told you so' look and I smile politely as Maria pours us all a glass of wine. She bustles out of the room and reappears minutes later with a small wooden trolley, which rattles as she pushes it up the room from the doorway. I stifle a giggle and can't look at Joe because the whole situation strikes me as ridiculous; from getting trapped in the snow to the lord of the manor rescuing us, it's like something out of a cheesy novel. Maria serves our starter and retreats with her rattly trolley and Evan orders us to *tuck in*.

Joe chats to Evan as we eat, but most of it goes over my head, as I'm not really listening. Stocks and shares are mentioned, but I zone out and concentrate on my food. Some sort of soup, sweet potato, I think. Occasionally I glance up at the two of them and disconcertingly, each time, Evan is staring right at me. His eyes are a very pale grey, his eyelashes almost transparent, and the thought strikes me that there's something reptilian about them. Joe is oblivious; he's already on his second glass of wine and is growing more garrulous by the minute; not drunk, but talking a lot, which is how too much alcohol affects him.

Maria reappears to clear the plates away, complete with trolley again, and replaces the empty bottle of wine with a fresh one, not smiling once while she does so. I realise that she's much younger than I at first thought, probably around my age, but her serious expression makes her seem older.

'So, Beth, although you're between jobs, what do you do when you're working?'

'I'm an accountant, the same as Joe.'

'Really? Two accountants married to each other. It surely can't be as dull as it sounds.' Evan laughs at his own joke and before I can answer, Joe cuts in.

'She wasn't always an accountant.'

I shoot Joe a warning look, astonished at what he's just said. We don't talk about what I used to do; it's private and not up for discussion.

Maria suddenly appears at the side of me and slides a plate of beef casserole onto the table in front of me, making me jump.

'Really?' Evan raises his eyebrows.

'She used to work in the media,' Joes says.

'That was years ago,' I say quickly, before Joe can say anything else. 'I'm between jobs at the moment, but I intend to find a new challenge once I'm fighting fit again.'

'Beth has been temping for the last few years

because she's still looking for the right permanent position.' Joe says. 'That's how we met. She came to temp at the company I work for.'

'So you worked in the media? Sounds interesting.' Evan says, refusing to let it go. 'I'm intrigued.'

'She worked for her father. Managed his public appearances and stuff for him. You've probably heard of him. James Winters.' Joe's positively beaming and right now, I could slap him. Why is he telling Evan this? We don't ever talk about my dad with other people and Joe had always known and respected this.

'What, *the* James Winters?' Evan asks.

'Yep. CEO and owner of The Winters Group.'

I concentrate on my food, but I can feel Evan's eyes on me and practically hear the cogs of his brain whirring. I'm in shock that Joe has told him this and we're going to be having words about this later. Everyone knows James Winters because he's often in the news, flashing his money around, supporting fashionable causes and mixing with the rich and famous. Just like Richard Branson, Dad likes to be noticed and would go to the opening of an envelope.

'So you're Lizzi Winters?' Evan asks.

'No,' I snap. 'I was Lizzi Winters but I'm Beth Coburn now.'

He snaps his fingers, looking pleased with himself. 'I knew I recognised you. I never forget a face. You always used to accompany him, didn't you, to the celebrity events?'

I don't answer, because I don't need to. Thanks to Joe, Evan will now see me as the socialite daughter of James Winters; a vapid airhead who lived her life in a social whirl as soon as she was old enough to wear a pair of designer stilettos. Someone who was gifted a job with no effort at all of her own.

'She likes to keep it a secret,' Joe says with a smirk as he drains the last of the wine from his glass. 'I had no idea who she was when I met her and she didn't tell me for months.'

'It's not a secret,' I say. 'It's just that it was years ago and is no longer relevant. I've moved on. I'm a different person now. I'm an accountant.'

'Why did you change your name?'

'I didn't. My name is Elizabeth which was shortened to Lizzi but now I go by Beth. When I got married, I took Joe's name.'

'I didn't recognise her,' Joe says, as Maria tops up his glass again. 'Because she looks completely different now, doesn't she? Better, I think, because she's naturally beautiful and doesn't need all that artifice. And she always talks herself down, don't you, Beth? I mean, your dad wouldn't have got half as much attention from the media if he hadn't had you on his arm.'

Joe sits back and drinks his wine, looking pleased with himself. No one else would notice, but I can tell he's had too much to drink. His words are slurring slightly and his eyes have a glassy look.

And his mouth has run away with him.

'So what prompted you to move out of the public eye, Beth, or should I say, Lizzi?' Evan smiles at me.

'Like I said, I wanted a change. A new direction in life. It was fun while it lasted, but I wanted to move on.'

'And your father, how did he feel about it when you suddenly decided that you wanted a new life?'

'He was fine about it.' I pick up my glass of wine and take several large gulps, swallowing the wine down with the lie I just told, because it couldn't be further from the truth.

◆ ◆ ◆

Joe's already in bed when I come out of the bathroom after cleaning my teeth. His eyes are closed and he's gently snoring, but I speak loudly to wake him up because I'm not about to let him get away with talking about my dad with Evan.

'Thanks for that, Joe.'

'What?' He opens his eyes and looks up at me in confusion as I clamber into bed.

'For blabbing to Evan about my Dad.'

He turns over on his side to face me and grins.

'Sorry. Got a bit carried away.'

'That'll be all the wine you glugged.'

'Yeah, maybe. It doesn't matter though, does it? I mean, he is your dad and Evan already said he recognised you.'

'So what? I don't see why you have to talk about him. You don't bring up your family, do you? In fact, you never talk about them.'

'Well, it's different, isn't it? My parents are dead and I lost touch with the rest of my family years ago. And they're not exactly anything to brag about; still stuck in the same place they were born in and a complete bunch of dull arses. No ambition. Nothing. They're hardly interesting.'

'Nor is my dad.'

'Not to you, but to other people he is. It's not just that he's stinking rich, he's got a big personality and everyone knows who he is. I don't get you; I'd be proud if he was my dad. I don't know why we have to keep him a big secret from all our friends either, you should have had my upbringing and then you'd have something to moan about.'

We've had this discussion many times; Joe doesn't understand my need for privacy, nor that I don't want the entire world to know who I, or rather, my dad, is.

'I don't like talking about him because people see me differently when you tell them. They don't see me as a person, they see me as a trust fund kid. A rich, spoilt brat who's never done a day's work in her life and I'm not that person anymore. It's not who I am now.'

'We're never going to see Evan again after this weekend so who cares what he knows or what he thinks?'

'I just don't see why you have to talk

about it. Boasting about my dad makes me feel uncomfortable.'

'Christ, Beth, this is the only time I've ever mentioned him and yeah, I got carried away but where's the harm? None of our friends know who your dad is, do they? Even my best mate has no idea who my wife really is because I'm not allowed to tell him. So I'm not a blabbermouth, despite what you say.'

'So why tell Evan?'

'I don't know, I was enjoying myself, I suppose, got carried away. Come on.' He puts his arm around me and pulls me closer. 'Forget about it. It's not important.'

'I'm not happy with you, Joe.'

'You could pretend to be Lizzi for the night. Do a bit of role play.' He grins. 'Put some of her designer gear on, do the lips. Go on, pucker up.'

'Shut up,' I say. 'Not funny.'

'Lizzi's hot. Almost as hot as Beth. I could pretend to be someone else, too. It'd be fun.'

Twisting out of his arms, I turn off the bedside light, plunging us into darkness.

'Go to sleep. It's late and I'm done in.'

'Spoilsport,' Joe mutters.

Staring into the darkness, the sound of Joe's steady breathing soon tells me he's asleep. It's been a long day but I know that sleep won't come easily now. The talk of my past has stirred up memories of my old life and old friends.

Of Quinn.

When I told Joe that I'm a different person now, I wasn't lying. Evan insists he recognised me, but I don't see how he could. I look nothing like I used to.

I struggle to recognise myself.

Dad still can't understand my desire to distance myself from the world he lives in; my insistence that I lead a normal life and not one where money is everything. He did his utmost to dissuade me from leaving Lizzi behind, telling me he needed me by his side, but I was adamant. I no longer wanted that life.

Because how can you ever be sure if people want you for who you are or just for your money?

You can't.

Quinn fooled me; he convinced me he loved me and I gave all that love and more back to him, but he was cheating on me. He never loved me at all. All he wanted was a ticket to the good life with my Dad's money. The hurt I felt was indescribable because I'd truly loved him and I tried so hard to be what he wanted; the glamourous outfits, the high maintenance hair, the perfectly made up girlfriend. When I wasn't seeing Quinn, I spend most of my life in beauty salons getting the latest trend; the new nails, the fake eyelashes, the filled lips. I'd been to university and qualified as an accountant, but I'd never even used my degree, because I lived my life for what I looked like, not what I could do.

But it wasn't only Quinn; I was tired of it all. To

begin with, it was exciting, and I loved the glitz and the glamour of going to events with Dad, but after a while the novelty wore off and it felt fake, hollow. It's different for Dad; he had many years of working hard to *get* that lifestyle and now he's reaping the rewards and enjoying the fruits of his labours, whereas I was just lucky enough to be born into it. I'm not ungrateful. I just want there to be more to my life than spending money and living a social whirl.

Closing my eyes, I try my old trick of mentally shoving these thoughts into a box and putting them away. It usually works, clearing my mind so I can sleep. It works this time, too, because soon my thoughts aren't of Dad, or my old life, but of Evan, our strange rescuer. There's something off about him, something that I don't like but can't put my finger on. I should be grateful to him for rescuing us from the blizzard, but my only thought as I drift off to sleep is that I'll be glad when tomorrow comes and we can leave this house.

CHAPTER FIVE

Daylight seeps through a small gap where the curtains don't quite meet, casting a sliver of brightness across the room. My phone confirms it's gone eight o'clock – I'm stunned that I've slept so late. Normally, if I stay asleep until six-thirty, it feels like a victory.

Lying still under the warmth of the heavy duvet, I listen to the steady rhythm of Joe's breathing. He always says he could sleep on a washing line, and I believe him. He has a knack for sleeping and will stay that way until I, or the alarm, wake him from his dreams. Sleep is something that I struggle with and I envy his ability to sleep anywhere, at any time. When I tell him it's because he has a clear conscience and leads a guilt-free life, he thinks I'm joking. Which I sort of am, except that he *is* totally honest and up front and that must help, mustn't it? Despite Joe over-sharing with Evan last night, his open nature is one of the things that made me fall in love with him.

That, and his good looks, obviously.

He likes to pretend he's a computer nerd, but he certainly doesn't look like one; even asleep, he's gorgeous; thick, dark hair that has a natural wave, skin that always looks tanned, and a body honed to perfection at the gym. I'd have fallen for him anyway, but the fact that he had no clue who I was sealed it for me. He loves me for who I am, and not for what he can get out of me.

Or rather, from my dad.

Pushing back the duvet, I lean down, grab my crutches from the floor, strap on my walking boot and head to the bathroom, pausing midway to peer out of the bedroom window. Outside, the world is blanketed in white, but the snow has stopped falling. That means we can leave today, get our car recovered and go home, or if Joe insists, continue to the hotel. I'm not sure if it's worth the trouble, considering we'll be going home tomorrow, anyway. There's no way our car will get fixed today because garages don't work on a Sunday. I carry on to the bathroom and by the time I return, showered and dressed, Joe is awake, sitting up in bed, staring at his phone.

'Still no signal,' he mutters, frowning.

'We'll have to use Evan's landline to ring a garage,' I say. 'Or we could log on to his Wi-Fi. This place is obviously a dead zone for mobile coverage.'

Joe tosses his phone onto the bedside table with a sigh. 'I wonder what's for breakfast? Last night's dinner was excellent. Maria can certainly cook, despite being miserable.'

'A piece of toast will do me.'

'If there's a feast on offer, I'm not saying no.'

'Pig.'

'I'm a growing boy.' He grins, stretching his arms above his head. 'Don't you think this house is incredible? It's probably better than the hotel we were going to stay at. It's even got a pool. You brought your swimmers, didn't you?'

'Yes, but we're leaving, aren't we?'

'Yeah, but why look a gift horse in the mouth? Evan said we're welcome to use it, and it'll take a while to get someone out to tow the car. Might as well enjoy ourselves.'

'Mick could give us a lift to the next village, though, couldn't he? Or maybe even the hotel. Let's offer to pay him. We could leave our car keys with him for when the tow truck turns up so we don't have to wait around for it.'

'Hmm.' He looks thoughtful. 'That'll look really ungrateful doing that when Evan's been so welcoming. As if we're desperate to get away.'

I am desperate to get away. The thought of hanging around here doesn't appeal to me at all.

'What's your problem with Evan?' Joe asks with a frown. 'He seems like a nice guy. Not everyone would be so welcoming.' He clambers out of bed and saunters to the bathroom.

'I haven't got a problem,' I say to his retreating back. 'I just want to get our car fixed and get to the hotel. Or go home.'

Joe doesn't reply and continues into the bathroom, closing the door firmly. Not quite a slam, but getting there.

What is my problem?

I don't know.

I just know that I don't feel comfortable here and that something about Evan is off.

Or maybe my overly suspicious nature is taking over again or, as Joe sometimes says, I'm being a princess. Not everyone is after something. There are lots of genuinely nice people around, I remind myself. Besides, what could Evan possibly want from us? Until yesterday, he'd never set eyes on us, so why am I making such a big deal about staying here for a few more hours?

Lighten up, Beth; lose the paranoia. Stop making it all about you.

Is that what I'm doing? For most of my life, I've been very aware of who I am, but my life is different now; I'm not that person anymore.

When Joe returns from the bathroom, I make a determined effort to be upbeat and not negative. I've unpacked our swimming gear and laid it out on the bed to show willing. Joe glances at it but doesn't comment as he sits down to put his shoes on.

When we get downstairs to the dining room, we're greeted by an array of covered silverware on the sideboard along one wall, which, judging by the smell, contains a cooked breakfast. There are three places set at the table, but no sign of Evan.

What's the etiquette? Do we help ourselves, or wait for him?

'Do you want me to get you something? It might be difficult trying to serve yourself holding those crutches,' Joe offers.

'Please.' I settle myself down in a chair. 'Do you think we should wait for Evan?'

'Help yourselves,' Evan says as he strides into the room. 'Forgive me for not being here to greet you. I've just been checking on the weather. It's snowing again, I'm afraid. Heavily.' He joins Joe at the sideboard, picks up a plate, takes the covers off the food and heaps bacon and sausages onto his plate.

'What's the forecast?' Joe asks.

'More of the same, apparently. For once, us soft southerners are getting it all while the north is getting the rain.'

Joe puts a plate down in front of me; bacon, two sausages and a poached egg.

'Is that enough? Do you want toast, too?' he asks.

'No, this is plenty. Thank you.' I reach for the jug in the centre of the table, pouring myself a glass of fresh orange juice before taking a sip.

'Did you both sleep well?' Evan asks.

'Like a log,' Joe replies.

'Beth?' Evan turns his gaze to me, his pale eyes staring at me coolly.

'I did too. 'It's a very comfortable bed. You have a beautiful home, Evan, and it's very kind of you to let us stay.'

He watches me for a moment before giving a small nod. 'Good. I'm glad you're comfortable. You're welcome to stay as long as you need and, of course, as I was saying to Joe last night, you must make use of the pool while you're here.'

'Thank you.'

'Yeah,' Joe says, as he spears a sausage with his fork. 'We've got our swimmers out ready. Have to work off this delicious breakfast, don't we, Beth?'

'Definitely.' I lower my head and even though I'm not at all hungry, I eat. The food is excellent, as Joe says, as good as any hotel, but I have to force down every mouthful. It's not the food that unsettles me, it's Evan. Because every time I glance up, he's watching me.

Joe and Evan keep up a stream of conversation as we eat and I join in occasionally, reminding myself to smile and seem at ease because I don't want Joe to know how badly I want to get out of here.

Finally, after what seems like forever, Joe asks the question I've been wanting to know the answer to since I got in here.

'So, Evan, could I use your landline? Neither Beth nor I have a signal on our mobiles and I need to ring the breakdown company.'

'You won't get a signal here,' Evan says. 'This house is dead to the mobile world and I'm afraid my landline stopped working yesterday, too. It happens occasionally when we have bad weather.

Last time it went off, it was out for weeks and I'm not a priority, as I'm the only house for miles.'

'Don't you have Wi-Fi?' I ask.

'We do. I'll ask Maria to give you the code.'

'Thank you.'

'But in the meantime, why don't you enjoy the house? Have a swim, the pool is heated. We have a sauna, too.'

'Wow, a sauna! We'll certainly take you up on that, won't we, Beth?'

'Sounds wonderful,' I say, forcing a smile.

Maria comes in with a fresh pot of coffee, busying herself with topping up our cups.

'Maria?' Evan asks. 'Could you find the code for the Wi-Fi and let our guests have it?'

'Of course.' She leaves the room, her face as impassive as when she came in. I glance at Joe and he rolls his eyes and pulls a face while staring at Maria as she leaves and I stifle a giggle, hoping that Evan hasn't noticed. Feeling suddenly light-hearted, I realise that Joe's right; we need to enjoy ourselves and make the most of the place while we're here. When Maria brings us the code, we can ring the breakdown people then have a swim and a sauna while we wait for them to arrive. Why do I always have to make everything so complicated with my 'weird feelings' about people?

Grow up, Beth, and stop thinking the worst.

◆ ◆ ◆

Getting into the rhythm of swimming, I discover it's surprisingly easy to swim whilst kicking only one leg. All the tension that I'd built up in my body after the events of yesterday has now gone and I decide that once my leg is fully healed, I'll start swimming regularly at the gym. Reaching the end of the pool, I grab hold of the side, intending to flip over and change to backstroke.

'You're enjoying this, aren't you?' Joe appears beside me, grinning.

'I am. I'd forgotten how much I love swimming.'

'You're practically a fish. Your dad's got a pool, hasn't he?'

'He has. Pretty much the same size as this one. I used to swim every day, without fail.'

'That's why you're such a good swimmer. I never learned to swim until I was fifteen. Taught myself at the local river.'

'And now you're nearly as good as me,' I joke.

'I'll never be as good as you.' Kicking off from the side, Joe heads towards the other end of the pool. We come from such different backgrounds; Joe doesn't say a lot about his upbringing, other than his parents weren't really interested in either him or his brothers. He seems embarrassed about the fact that he was poor even though it's nothing to be ashamed of. We have no control over what we're born into, do we? He often tells me I don't know how lucky I am to have had such a privileged upbringing and although I know he's right, he doesn't have all the facts; not everything about my childhood was wonderful. Money isn't everything. My mother died when I was very young, so I've never had a mother. I struggle to remember her and am uncertain whether my memories are genuine or if I've just imagined them based on what Dad's told me and the photographs I've seen. Are they actual memories or not? I was nearly three years old when she died. Would I remember from that young?

'Sauna?' Joe shouts from the other end of the pool, as he heaves himself out of the water.

'Yes,' I shout back. 'But I need your help to get out.' Kicking off with my good leg, I swim towards the steps. Hauling myself up and hopping up the steps on my good leg, Joe puts the crutches underneath my arms when I reach the top. It's strange to be upright again and I hop along behind him, missing the buoyancy of the water. Leaving the pool room, we go along a dark corridor to a sauna built into the end of the building. Once we're inside with the door closed, the heat is intense. Flopping down onto the wooden bench, I wonder how long I'll be able to stay in here.

'There's a cold shower next door,' Joe says.

'God, no. Are you trying to kill me?' I say, shuddering at the thought.

Fifteen minutes later and both of us burst out of the sauna, unable to stand it a moment longer, sweating and red-faced. We go back to our room – a long way in this enormous house – and get showered and dressed.

Maria has been in the room while we were swimming because although I made the bed, it's been remade with military precision; not a crease or rumpled sheet in sight. Fresh towels have been placed in the bathroom, and the sink and shower have been cleaned and dried.

But, annoyingly, she hasn't left us the Wi-Fi code.

'It's stopped snowing.' Gazing out of the window, I see the driveway is buried under a thick layer of snow, but the sky appears brighter and lighter so hopefully that's the end of the bad weather.

'I'll go and ask Maria for that code,' Joe says.

'I'll come,' I say, grabbing my crutches.

Once down in the hall, we stand looking at each other, slightly embarrassed, unsure of what to do. Where is Maria? Do we go looking for her, or find Evan? I opt for sitting on one of the two sofas that sit opposite the front door while Joe goes to look for her. We *think* the corridor next to the dining room leads to the kitchen, so Joe heads off that way. As I wait for him, I realise how lost I am without my mobile phone. Normally, right now I'd be looking at it, scrolling through social media, looking at emails or reading the news online. Like most people, it's my go to activity whenever I have a spare few minutes and without it in my hand, I feel cut off from life. Being without it has been an eye-opener, even after such a short time. Maybe both Joe and I should think about switching our mobiles off now and again, having some time every day without them because it's surely not good to be so dependent on them.

The sound of talking catches my attention. The door to the lounge is ajar, and I lean forward and catch sight of Evan through the gap. He's standing by the window, deep in conversation, his phone clamped to his ear. Even though I can't make out what he's saying, I feel awkward, as if I'm eavesdropping, even though it's completely unintentional. At that instant, he turns away from the window and looks in my direction. I hurriedly look away and lean back against the sofa, wondering if he's seen me. When I hear the door close with a click, I know he has, and my cheeks burn with embarrassment.

Joe comes down the corridor from the kitchen and walks quickly towards me.

'Christ, that was hard work,' he says, quietly, as I get up. 'Talk about socially awkward. It's as if speaking is actually painful for her.'

'You've got the code, though?'

He sighs. 'No, I haven't. The bloody internet's gone down, hasn't it? No landline and now no broadband either. Just our luck.'

'No internet?'

'Nope. It went down a couple of hours ago. Maria said that the last time it happened, it was off for nearly a week. It's not like they can even report it because there's no way to contact the provider. So there's no way we can ring a garage.'

I stare at Joe, trying to make sense of his words.

If there's no internet, how was Evan using his phone a few minutes ago?

CHAPTER SIX

Joe's gone to speak to Evan and I'm back on the sofa, waiting for him to come back.

Did I imagine Evan using his phone? Was I mistaken?

No. The door was only slightly open, but he was definitely speaking and he had his phone clamped to his ear, I could see that much.

Why would Maria lie about the internet not working? The unease that I've felt since meeting Evan, resurfaces. I haven't said anything to Joe about seeing Evan using his phone, but as soon as we're back in the privacy of our room, I'll be telling him.

Joe and Evan come out of the lounge and walk towards me, smiling and chatting as if they're old friends.

'Such a nuisance about the internet being down. Very tiresome. Did you enjoy your swim?' Evan asks me with a smile.

'I did. It's such a lovely pool and the sauna

afterwards was perfect.' *Why are you lying, Evan?*

'It is a good sized pool although, to my shame, I don't use it nearly enough. I'm afraid.'

'Evan's going to speak to Mick, see if he can tow us to the nearest village,' Joe says.

'That would be great.'

'I'll find him and ask him about it now. Hopefully, he's in the garage, but you never know with Mick. There's a library full of books if you're bored, but I can't vouch for any of them as I'm not a reader, but it may help pass the time.' He goes to a doorway next to the dining room and opens it wide. 'Maria's making us some lunch for one o'clock, but if you want a drink or anything in the meantime, just ask her.'

There's an awkward pause and I realise that they're waiting for me to get up. Gathering my crutches, I cross to the library and go inside. Joe doesn't follow but walks away with Evan and I realise he's going with him to speak to Mick. Feeling insulted at being treated like the little woman, I remind myself I'm on crutches, so don't want to be hobbling around in the snow, but even knowing that, I can't shake off my annoyance.

To distract myself, I look around the vast room, its walls lined with shelves overflowing with books. I've no desire to read anything or have any lunch. I just want to pack my bags and leave. But now we're expected to stay for lunch, dragging things out even further. It's nearly midday, which means we're stuck here for at least another couple of hours. Sighing with impatience, I select a book at random from the shelf and flop down onto a large sofa.

Hurry up and sort it out, Joe. I want to go home.

The book is an Agatha Christie mystery and judging by the dust; it hasn't been read in a very long time. Staring at the words without even seeing them, I fume with Joe and Evan for excluding me. The minutes tick by, literally, a gigantic clock on the mantelpiece ticking so loudly that I count every one of them. Time drags painfully slowly and I wonder what can be taking them so long. When Joe finally appears in the doorway, flushed in the face from the cold air, it's ten to one.

'Lunch is nearly ready, you coming?'

Opening my mouth to ask him when we're leaving, I close it again because he's already gone, shrugging off his coat on his way. It looks as if I'm going to have to eat lunch whether I want to or not. So much for a romantic weekend away; the only love here is the bromance between Joe and Evan. I get up and make my way to the dining room. Walking is getting a lot easier now, and the swimming did my leg some good. I think I could manage now with just one crutch.

Again, the table is set with three places and the sideboard is filled with a buffet that would feed ten people. Evan must keep a very full larder to be able to cater for unexpected guests like us. He's already seated in his usual spot, opening a bottle of wine.

'Tuck in,' he says. 'Although Maria has rather overdone it.' He smiles and again, I'm reminded of a reptile.

'Hungry?' Joe asks.

'Not really.'

'I am, I'm starving. Must be that swimming. Shall I get you a plateful?'

'No, it's okay, I think I can manage.' Leaning one of my crutches up against the table, I walk to the sideboard and pick up a plate with my free hand. Soon discovering that it's awkward to load my plate one-handed, I don't ask Joe for help because I'm pissed off with him. He keeps glancing at me as he helps himself to food, but I ignore him and after watching me for a while, he sits down without offering help again.

Just tell me when we're leaving Joe, and stop sucking up to the weirdo lord of the manor.

'So, good news and bad news.' Joe says as I sit down at the table opposite him.

'Okay.' I don't like the sound of that.

'It is,' Evan says smoothly. 'The bad news is that Mick tells us the weather is still too bad to tow your car, even though it's stopped snowing now. The good news is that the forecast is for it to thaw tomorrow, so all being well, he'll be able to tow you to the village then.'

Which means we have to stay another night.

'Perhaps we could leave the car here and Mick could give us a lift in his truck,' I suggest. 'It's massive, isn't it? It didn't have any trouble bringing us here yesterday, and the weather was much worse then.'

Joe glances at me and frowns. Maybe the words came out more sharply than I intended; I never meant to be rude, but you know what? Too bad. I want to leave, and this just sounds like yet another excuse to me. Maybe Evan is lonely and enjoys having some company, but I don't want to spend another night here.

'That is true,' Evan says. 'But that was an emergency because he could hardly leave you both to freeze in the car, could he? It would be too risky to both Mick and the vehicle and whilst I understand you're eager to be on your way, it's not an emergency, is it?'

'Of course it's not,' Joe says hurriedly. 'And it's very good of you to be so hospitable, Evan. You're just disappointed about our getaway, aren't you, Beth?' he says, turning to me.

He's embarrassed and apologising for me now.

'I am.' I lie. 'I was so looking forward to our romantic weekend away, and now we're never going to get there. I'm sorry if I sounded ungrateful Evan, like Joe says, it's very good of you to put us up and I hope I haven't offended you.'

'Not at all. I'm afraid I can't offer you much in the way of facilities, but please make yourselves at home whilst you're here. Thankfully, the television in the lounge still works as it's run on satellite and not internet based. There are bonuses to being a Luddite.' He laughs and Joe joins in and after a moment, I do, too, because I'm stuck here and don't want to look like a complete misery. 'The Grand Prix is on this afternoon, Joe, and you're very welcome to join me. Fortunately, there's no snow in Bahrain. And you too, of course, Beth, if you're interested.'

'Definitely be up for that,' Joe says. 'Motor sport is one of my passions although Beth will give it a miss, won't you?' He grins at me.

'I'll pass. Truthfully, I'd rather stick pins in my eyes.' *And I'm not really wanted, am I? Because they've made that pretty obvious.*

'Well, there's always the library.' Evan smiles.

Of course, the library.

What fun.

◆ ◆ ◆

'You're being ridiculous.' Joe hisses at me.

We're in our room, dressed, ready to go down for dinner. I've been up here for hours trying, and failing, to read one of the books I took from the library. Joe's been in the lounge watching the F1 with Evan all afternoon and came back only twenty minutes ago. He went straight into the bathroom, telling me we'd be late for dinner if we didn't hurry, as if I'm the one who'd been lounging around watching TV all afternoon.

'I'm ready,' I snapped at him. 'Whereas you're not.'

When he came out of the bathroom and started

getting dressed, I told him about Evan's phone call. He never said a word until I'd finished speaking and then gave a big sigh and looked at me as if I had two heads.

And told me I was being ridiculous.

'No, I'm not. I saw him through the gap in the door. He was standing by the window, talking to someone on his phone. I saw him and I heard him. I didn't imagine it.'

'You're mistaken.' Joe says. 'The internet isn't working.'

'Maybe Evan is lying about that.'

'Why would he lie?' He laughs. 'What possible reason could he have for lying?'

'I don't know, but I know what I saw.'

'You're wrong.'

'I'm not.'

'Again, why?' Joe sighs. 'We're the ones staying here for free and getting treated like we're staying at a five-star hotel. What's Evan getting out of it? Nothing, that I can see. I don't know what your problem is. Someone is nice to us and you go all paranoid and accuse him of lying about the bloody internet.'

'So I'm lying?'

'No. Wrong word. Sorry. You're mistaken, that's all. The door was only slightly open, wasn't it? You said that yourself. You couldn't see properly and your brain filled in the gaps incorrectly.' He pulls open the bedroom door, staggering slightly as the door sticks in the ancient doorframe.

'Have you been drinking?'

He shrugs. 'Just a couple of beers.'

'With your new best mate,' I state.

He turns, blocking the doorway.

'Oh, I see.' His eyes narrow as he studies me. 'I get it now. You're jealous, aren't you?'

'Jealous? What would I be jealous of?'

'Evan. Because I spent the afternoon watching sport with him instead of spending time with you. You could have sat with us, you know. Joined in. Been sociable.'

'Now you're being ridiculous. No way am I jealous. And anyway, I don't want to sit with him. He's creepy.'

'Shush,' he hisses. 'Keep your voice down. He might hear you. What's wrong with you? He's been good enough to put us up and feed us and all you've done is complain. Stay up here and I'll say you're not well or something if you can't stand his company.'

'I'm hungry.' I'm not.

'Well then, Slap a smile on your face and see if you can be pleasant. *Princess*.'

He strides off down the landing, giving me no opportunity to reply. Seething, I follow behind, fighting the urge to fling one of the crutches at his back. I am *not* a princess and Joe knows that; he's only said it because he knows that it absolutely incenses me.

And I didn't imagine Evan using his phone. I know what I saw.

Joe doesn't wait for me to catch up with him and by the time I've clattered down the stairs and into the dining room, he's already seated at the table with Evan. They're deep in conversation and it's only as I pull the chair out to sit down that they both glance up, giving me the feeling that they've been talking about me.

Forcing myself to smile, I manoeuvre myself into my seat, feeling distinctly uncomfortable.

Joe wouldn't be so disloyal, would he?

Before today I would have said he absolutely wouldn't, but for some reason he seems to hang on Evan's every word and won't have a thing said against him. How can he not believe me when I tell him what I saw?

'Joe tells me you thought you saw me using a mobile phone,' Evan says calmly.

I stare at him, and then Joe, trying to hide my horror. He's *told* him.

'And I'm sure you must have thought that strange as the internet isn't working, but although it may have looked like a phone, it was a recorder. I use it for dictation for my business ventures, a reminder to myself, rather better than a notebook, as my handwriting is appalling.'

'Evan is a venture capitalist,' Joe says, beaming, clearly oblivious to the fact that right now, I'd like to kill him.

My face feels so hot that I could probably start a fire if I wanted to.

'I thought it must be something like that,' I lie,

wincing at how pathetic I sound.

'Dinner's going to be a little delayed, so how about we have a cocktail to start? It's my own recipe, which I can't reveal, but you won't be disappointed.' Evan gets up and busies himself at the sideboard, opening the cupboard beneath and taking out glasses, bottles of spirits, and a battered cocktail shaker.

Joe looks at me, and I glare back at him. He stares at me innocently, as if he has no idea what he's done. Really? Is he that dense? He couldn't have embarrassed me more if he'd tried.

Evan brings our cocktails to the table and I take a tentative sip. I'm pretty sure it has whisky in it. Yuk. It's heady, strong and chock full of alcohol. Instant headache and hangover material. I put it down on the table and wish it would magically disappear into thin air.

'Don't you like it?' Evan asks.

'It's lovely.'

'Well, drink up.' He raises his glass in the air and Joe does the same.

'Cheers.' Evan holds my gaze, staring steadily at me and feeling forced to join in, I pick up the glass.

'You're quite safe, you know,' he says. 'It's not poisoned.'

Joe bursts out laughing and Evan joins in as if what he's said is hilarious. Giving a smile that I don't mean, I force down the disgusting mixture by swallowing it in big gulps as quickly as possible because I have no choice but to drink it. When I put the glass down on the table, I swear to God I feel drunk already.

Maria comes in carrying a tray with our starters on and, suddenly starving, I concentrate on eating the duck pate she puts in front of me, hopeful that it'll soak up the alcohol. Joe and Evan are talking about financial markets now, and I'm surprised and slightly impressed by Joe's knowledge of them.

My earlier anger at him is fading. Was I overreacting?

Maybe. Possibly. We can talk about it later, when we're on our own, but for now, I just want to get through this dinner and escape back up to our room. The main course arrives and I'm halfway through eating the lemon sole when I realise that I'm no longer hungry. I'm not full but suddenly have no appetite at all and every mouthful of the fish feels like cardboard in my mouth and I'm having trouble swallowing. Putting down my knife and fork, I'm shocked to see that my hands are shaking.

'You okay, Beth?' Joe is looking at me from across the table, a concerned look on his face. 'You look really pale.'

'I don't feel very well.' I'm suddenly so hot that my skin feels as if it's on fire and I want to rip off my clothes.

'What's wrong?' He reaches across and takes hold of my hand. 'Christ, you're freezing.'

'I think I'm coming down with something.'

'You don't look good at all.'

I push the plate away because the smell of the food is making me want to vomit.

'Sorry to disrupt dinner,' I say, my voice wobbly. 'But I feel really unwell. I think I'm going to have to go to bed.' Evan is looking at us now and I feel sweat break out on my top lip.

'Hey come on, I'll take you up to the room,' Joe says, standing up.

'No, honestly, sit down. There's no need to spoil your dinner, too. I'll be okay as soon as I've had a lie down.' I stand up on shaky legs and grab my crutches. I just want to get out of here before I throw up all over the table.

Walking out to the hall with as much dignity as I can muster, I wonder why I'm so concerned about what I look like. Somehow I get myself up what seems like a never ending flight of stairs. With relief, I close the bedroom door behind me, stagger to the bed and lower myself down onto it. Once I've removed my walking boot and shoe, I crawl underneath the duvet, not caring one bit that I'm still wearing my clothes and makeup. As my head hits the pillow, my brain feels as though it's shaking and I lie as still as possible to stop it. Taking deep breaths, I swallow the nausea down because I don't feel capable of making it to the bathroom.

Just my luck to be ill and catch some bloody virus. Or maybe this is a migraine; I've never had one before, but I've heard people talk about them.

What else can go wrong on this disastrous

weekend?

My last thought as I drift off to sleep is that come what may, no matter how I feel in the morning, no matter what excuses Joe and Evan come up with, I'm going home first thing tomorrow morning.

Even if I have to walk there on my sodding crutches.

CHAPTER SEVEN

When I open my eyes, my first thought is how surprisingly okay I feel. Not amazing, because I have a headache and feel hungover, but it's nothing compared to how ill I felt last night. Was it that cocktail? It was strong and definitely had whisky in it, which I always avoid like the plague, but is that what made me feel so bad? I genuinely thought that I'd wake this morning with full-blown flu or a nasty virus that would incapacitate me for days.

But I feel okay.

And incredibly, I slept right through the night without waking once; practically unheard of for me. It also seems like I haven't moved at all from when I collapsed into bed last night. My body feels stiff and as if I haven't moved position all night. The black tights around my legs are rumpled, my dress feels like a rag and my bra straps are digging into my skin.

Time to hit the shower.

I turn over, my body aching in unexpected places as I do so, expecting to see Joe beside me. I'm met with a plump pillow and a smooth duvet where he should be. Pulling myself upright, I look at the bathroom door and see that it's open, so he's not in there, either. Joe never gets up before me, which means it must be really late. That also means I've overslept – something else I never do.

I look around for my phone. It may be useless for making calls but is still useful for checking the time. I can't see it anywhere. Where did I leave it? Last night is a blur. I haven't been taking it with me anywhere because it doesn't work, but have been leaving it on the bedside table. Either I moved it, or Joe, ever the neat freak, has tidied it away. Not that it really matters – I need to get up, shower, get dressed, and be ready to leave.

Swinging my legs onto the edge of the bed, I strip off my tights, pull the dress over my head, and toss both onto the bed before reaching for my crutches. On my way to the bathroom, I pause by the window. Dark patches peek through the snow. It's melting fast. Evan was right.

Which means we can get the car towed and go home as soon as I'm dressed. Feeling suddenly chipper at the thought of getting out of here, I grab some clothes from the open suitcase and go into the bathroom.

By the time I've showered, dressed and dried my hair, I'm feeling slightly guilty at my haste to escape this house. I haven't exactly been at my best since we've been here, and I probably should have shown more appreciation for Evan's generosity.

I definitely should have.

Would I have opened my home to strangers the way he has? No, I would not.

Maybe I am a bit of a princess. I try really hard not to be, constantly questioning myself over my behaviour to make sure I'm not being a brat. I can usually see clearly when I'm acting spoilt. My only excuse is that staying here wasn't planned, and I find Evan uncomfortable company, but that's no excuse for being ungracious. As soon as we're home, I'll arrange for a thank you gift for Evan, maybe flowers. Is that fitting for a man? Or a basket of fruit or similar to show him how grateful we are. Joe may want to keep in touch with him, because he gets on so well with him. I don't, but that's fine because we have friends of our own. We don't have to share them all.

Because whatever Joe says, there definitely is something creepy about Evan; something off about him.

Pulling on jeans and a thick jumper, I'm dressing for travel. There may be a problem getting a hire car if the nearest place is a village. It would be better if Mick took us to the nearest town. Or we could get a cab and save him the trouble and then we won't have to wait until he's available. I'm pretty sure our breakdown cover includes onward travel, so one way or another, we'll be getting home today.

Once I'm dressed, I pack everything back into the case, ready to leave. Weirdly, I still can't find my phone even though it must be in this room somewhere. Did I take it down to the pool with me, thinking I could get a signal? Perhaps I did. Once I'm downstairs, I'll ask Joe to have a look for me to save me the long trek.

Time to go.

Which is when I discover the door won't open; it's stuck and won't budge at all.

Almost as if it's locked.

There is a lock on it; an old-fashioned keyhole underneath the large brass door knob. Leaning down, I squint at it and see straight through onto the landing. Was there ever a key in it? I don't recall seeing a key, but I wasn't exactly looking. Why would it be locked?

It could be stuck. This house is old; wood swells and contracts with the temperature, doesn't it? Maybe the rise in temperature from the thaw has made the wood swell and the door stick in the frame. It's possible. Grabbing hold of the handle, I turn it, but the door won't move at all. I pull with as much power as I can, holding onto the door frame for support.

Nothing.

And then it hits me; this odd feeling that I've had from the moment I stepped into this house, the thing that I couldn't shake off and kept telling myself was a reaction to Evan's weird manner.

The uneasy feeling that I couldn't, or wouldn't,

put a name to.

Fear.

◆ ◆ ◆

I'm calm. I am.

To prove it, I'm sitting on the bed and thinking it all through sensibly. No hysterics, no banging on the door, no screaming to be let out. There's absolutely no need to be afraid. It's just my imagination running away with me.

Maybe this is a kind of sick joke; Joe getting his own back on me for behaving like a princess. Teaching me a lesson. Locking me in the room like a naughty child.

No. He wouldn't do that to me because he knows I wouldn't find being locked in a room the least bit funny and Joe isn't spiteful like that; he's kind, considerate. But maybe Evan would find it funny. Perhaps he got Joe drunk and persuaded him to lock me in to teach me a lesson for being ungrateful for his generous hospitality and accusing him of lying about the Wi-Fi.

Yes, that'll be it. An unfunny joke from a creep of a man who spends far too much time alone.

Okay, if it is a joke, it's over now. I'll even pretend to find it funny when he lets me out because we're going home today and I'll never have to see that lizard-like smile again.

So I'm going to have to bang on the door, because it's my only option. The problem is, this house is huge. They might not even hear me from downstairs. Or maybe they're hiding on the landing, waiting for me to start shouting. So they can laugh at me, panicking and crying to be let out. Joe would feel that he had to go along with it; I expect he feels awkward because we're staying in Evan's house and he feels obliged to do what Evan suggests. Whatever, it doesn't matter. I just need to get out of here.

I knock on the door with my fist. It doesn't seem very loud, so I shout, too. Not 'help', but 'Joe', because 'help' would sound overly-dramatic. This must be a misunderstanding or a pathetic joke.

Yeah, like the internet not working.

I bang harder and shout louder, stopping now and then to hear if anyone is outside.

Silence.

Where the hell is Joe?

I eventually stop banging on the door because my knuckles are hurting. I tried using my left hand but couldn't get the required pressure to make enough noise. It should have been the same using a different hand, but somehow it wasn't.

Okay, what next?

The window. We're on the second floor but I can open the window and shout for help and if Joe and Evan aren't outside, Mick might be wandering around and hear me. Or Maria. It seems as if Mick spends a lot of time in the grounds, so if he's out there, he'll hear me shouting and if he doesn't, his dogs will. I'm pretty sure that dogs have extra good hearing. Or is that smell? I don't know.

Drawing the curtains fully back from the window, I look out. There's no one out there, just Mick's enormous truck parked on the sweeping gravel drive in front of the house. Was it parked there earlier when I looked out? I can't remember, but I don't think so because I'm sure I'd have noticed because it's so huge. Not that it matters. Grasping hold of the wooden sash, I attempt to push it up. It doesn't budge, so I push harder because it most likely hasn't been opened for years.

Nothing.

Which isn't surprising, because when I look more closely, there are painted over screwheads on either side of the catch, which means it's sealed shut. There's no way this window is opening.

The sound of the door being unlocked floods me with relief and grabbing one crutch, I turn towards the door, expecting to see Joe, but it's not him, it's Maria.

'Maria...'

She doesn't acknowledge me but puts the tray she has in her hands on the floor, avoiding meeting my eyes. I walk towards her, wondering what she's doing, but she's already pulling the door closed. I reach my hand out to the door handle at the same moment that I hear the click of the lock.

She's locked me in!

Even as my brain tells me this, it doesn't stop me from trying to pull the door open. It won't move. I bang on the door and shout her name, but there's no response.

'Not funny!' I shout through the door. 'Not funny at all. The joke is over now!'

Silence. I shout Joe's name, over and over again, and by the time I stop, my throat is hoarse.

What the hell is going on?

I sit down on the bed, my eyes falling on the tray Maria has put on the floor. A bottle of water and a plate of sandwiches. As I sit staring at it, voices from outside the window catch my attention. Instantly alert, I jump up, grab my crutches and rush to the window.

Mick and Evan are standing in the driveway, their heads close, their expressions serious. Evan turns his head towards the house and I raise my hand to bang on the window, but at that moment the dogs appear from behind the truck, barking wildly. Mick shouts at them and they stop barking, but they look alert, on guard, as if waiting for something.

Then Mick moves to the back of the truck, swinging open the doors. Evan turns and starts walking toward the house. I bang loudly on the window and call his name, but he doesn't react. He vanishes from view, and for a fleeting second, Mick looks up at me. But just as quickly, he looks away, unconcerned, as if hearing someone banging and shouting from the window is the most ordinary thing in the world.

The next moment, Evan reappears in the driveway, but he's not alone.

He's with Joe.

Evan is pushing Joe forward, his hand holding him by the back of his neck, forcing him toward Mick. My breath catches and I gasp in horror as I see that Joe's hands are bound behind him and there's a strip of cloth gagging his mouth. He staggers as Evan shoves him, struggling to keep his balance.

Stunned, I break out of my shock and slam both hands on the glass, shouting out Joe's name. My brain refuses to accept what I'm seeing; this can't be real; it has to be a nightmare.

'Joe!' I scream.

He turns his head and looks up at me for a second, and my hand flies to my mouth in horror. One of his eyes is blackened and bruised, and there's blood smeared around the gag covering his mouth. What the hell have they done to him?

Evan jerks him forward, and Joe stumbles, collapsing onto the ground. Without hesitation, Evan yanks him to his feet by one arm and drags him, stumbling, the rest of the way. When they reach the truck, Mick lifts Joe effortlessly onto his shoulder and throws him into the back of the truck like a discarded sack. My last glimpse of Joe is of his legs hanging over the edge before Mick picks them up and pushes them inside.

Then he calls the dogs.

I watch in growing terror as the dogs leap up into the truck after Joe and Mick slams the doors and locks them.

My God. Joe's in there with those beasts.

Tears spill down my face as I watch Mick climb into the cab and pull the door shut. Evan steps up beside the truck, speaking to him through the open window, and a moment later, the engine rumbles to life, and the truck lurches forward and heads off down the driveway.

Evan turns away, making his way back toward the house, and when he reaches the spot directly beneath my window, he stops and looks up at me.

And smiles.

CHAPTER EIGHT

I remained at the window, screaming at Evan long after he'd disappeared into the house. Apart from that cold smile, he never acknowledged me but simply stared at me for what felt like an eternity before finally lowering his gaze and retreating inside the house. I have no memory of when I stopped screaming or pounding on the glass, but I must have, because somehow, incredibly, I fell asleep.

When I awoke, I was lying on the floor by the window, and the room was in darkness. My throat burned with every swallow, my knuckles were cut and bloody, and my legs were twisted awkwardly beneath me. I had to massage them to restore the feeling before I attempted to crawl to the bed. Misjudging the distance, I banged my head against the bedside cabinet and saw stars for a moment. Hauling myself up onto the bed, I switched on the lamp and lay back, closing my eyes while I waited for the spinning sensation in my head to subside.

Jumbled thoughts have been tumbling through my mind ever since; where have they taken Joe and what are they going to do with him? Is he okay? What if the dogs attack him? But most of all.

Why?

None of it makes sense. I'm a prisoner and Joe has been taken somewhere and I don't know why. I disliked Evan on sight, but this madness? Why would he do this, whatever *this* is? What does he have in store for me? Sickness suddenly overwhelms me as nightmare scenarios of torture and rape push their way into my brain. I pull myself up into a sitting position and my head spins and I want to vomit. As I sob, the tears stream down my face, the taste of them salty in my mouth, and I can do nothing to stop myself from crying in despair.

I'm so frightened.

Do something about it.

It's Dad's voice in my head; his answer to every problem, no matter what it is, is to *do something about it.* He doesn't believe in waiting and seeing, in being passive. If something is wrong, you sort it out. Dad believes you make your own luck and your own future; that only you have control of your own destiny.

And isn't that how I've lived my life? It is; because that's how I met Joe.

So get up, Beth, take control and *do something.*

Except that I can't. I'm a prisoner and I have no control. I can't do anything except wait until Evan decides what he's going to do with me.

No, Dad's voice says in my head, there's always something you can do.

I take a deep breath and try to think straight. Okay, so I'm trapped in this room, but I have control over what I do while I'm in here; how I think, how I cope. I can lie on the bed and wallow, or I can use my brain to figure out how I'm going to get out of here and get help for Joe.

Thinking of Joe's face when he looked up at the window crushes me and the tears get worse again.

No. Stop. Crying won't help. Focus on what you have to do.

My crutches are lying on the floor by the window. To do anything, I need them. Sliding out of bed onto the floor, I drag myself over to them, grab hold of them, and pull them back to the side of the bed. Kneeling on my good leg, I haul myself onto the bed again, pull the crutches up and get upright. It's tiring but once upright on two feet, I feel better, more in control. I walk to the bedroom door and try the handle; it's still locked, of course. No change there. The tray that Maria brought in is still lying on the floor where she put it. I'm not in the least bit hungry, but I haven't eaten or drunk anything since last night. I've had nothing since I woke this morning. How long ago was that? A long time, because it gets dark at around five o'clock, and it's dark now, which means it's at least five o'clock or later. How many hours is that? I don't know, my head can't work it out, but it's too long without water, that's for sure. Perhaps if I force myself to eat, it'll help dispel the headache and dizziness. Starving myself will achieve nothing but make me weaker.

I need to be strong.

Using a crutch, I push the tray along the floor towards the bed, then sit down on the mattress. I drink half of the bottle of water and eat the sandwich. It's curled around the edges, but I force it down, taking swigs of water to help it down. When I've finished, I go into the bathroom and refill the bottle.

What now?

How long am I going to be left here?

I go over to the window and look outside. It's dark outside but Mick's truck is back, parked in the driveway. Have they brought Joe back? I hope so. Although why would they take him somewhere and then bring him back? That wouldn't make sense.

So many questions that I have no answers to, but common sense tells me that whatever Evan wants, at some point, I'm going to find out. There must be a reason this is happening, some rationale behind my imprisonment.

Unless Evan is a psycho and gets his kicks out of torturing and killing innocent couples, and there is no reason except his sadistic pleasure.

It's there again, the thought, and it's a terrifying one. I'm holding myself together right now because the alternative to that is falling apart.

But I'm trapped and imprisoned with only my thoughts to occupy me and torment myself with fear about what's going to happen to me and Joe.

Do something.

Turning from the window, I walk slowly up and down the room. After a while, I toss one crutch onto the bed and use only one. Walking becomes easier. My gait is steadier, surer, the pain in my leg bearable. I count my steps up and down the room, taking care not to lose track. It's important to keep my mind focussed so that the terror of what might happen can't take over. The pain in my leg increases and I consider taking painkillers to help. I have a packet in my wash bag. But I decide not; they make my head fuzzy and I need to keep my wits about me. Be sharp, alert.

It's tiring. My steps are getting slower, but I keep going because when I'm walking and counting, I'm not thinking about Joe and the terrible fate that could be in store for both of us.

Thinking won't help.

Keep walking, Beth, just keep walking.

◆ ◆ ◆

When I wake, again I have no idea what time it is. When I first open my eyes for the briefest of moments, my life is normal, unremarkable; Joe is beside me, fast asleep, and it's a day like any other. Reality crashes in within seconds and yesterday's events weigh so heavily that if I could, I would close my eyes and never wake up again, but of course, it's not that easy. Besides, I have hope that Joe and I can get out of this, whatever *this* is.

Daylight is streaming through the window. I never closed the curtains last night because the light is my only indication of time passing. I think about it and decide that it must be after seven o'clock because the mornings are dark until at least that time.

How lost I feel without a watch, a clock, or my mobile phone.

Getting out of bed and going into the bathroom, I use one crutch only. I'm finding it easy now, and although it hurts to walk, I ignore the pain. Collecting fresh underwear from my bag on the way, I decide I'll wear the same clothes as yesterday even though I've slept in them.

What will I do when I run out of clothes?

That won't happen, because I won't be here that long. I'm going to escape and get help.

Although how, I don't know.

Locking the bathroom door – laughable, as if it would keep Evan out – I shower and get dressed. Brush my teeth and hair and feel better for it. Joe's wash bag is still on the sink, as if he's just popped out and will be back at any moment. I open it and root through, pulling out his razor. He's brought his electric one, but this is an old-fashioned metal razor with a blade screwed inside. He never uses it; it was a long ago gift from a secret Santa and has been consigned to his wash bag instead of being thrown straight into the bin, where it belonged. Carefully unscrewing the metal handle, I take the two pieces apart, lift out the razor blade and place it on the basin surround. The metal is thin and lethally sharp.

What am I going to do with it?

Opening the door of the cabinet above the basin, I see it's empty except for a bar of soap and an empty glass. Taking out the bar of soap, I unwrap the paper from one end, pick up the razor and slide it in on top of the soap, and fold the paper back over. Putting it back into the cabinet, I place it at the end so that the open wrapper is pushed up against the wooden end of the cabinet and close the door.

No one will find it unless they're looking for it.

I screw the razor back together and return it to the wash bag. What am I going to do with the razor blade? Kill someone? I'll probably end up hurting myself. It's so sharp.

But it's something.

Opening my wash bag, I take out the nail scissors. They're quite sharp but so small I'm not sure how useful they'd be. I push them into the pocket of my jeans, unlock the bathroom door, and go into the bedroom. I could resume my walking because apart from keeping my mind focussed, my legs are my only means of escape, so I need to strengthen them. A sudden thought strikes me.

What if my every move is being watched? What if there are hidden cameras in this room, in the bathroom? Once the thought is there, it refuses to budge and, going back into the bathroom, I start to search. I have no idea what a secret camera looks like, but I look everywhere, scrutinising every tiny detail of the rooms. By the time I've finished, there's not an inch of the bathroom and bedroom that I haven't examined. Obviously I can't reach the ceiling, but surely a camera would stand out because there's nothing to conceal it? Hopefully, I'm right.

About to resume walking lengths of the room, the sound of someone outside the door stops me in my tracks and I hurriedly sit down on the side of the bed.

The door slowly opens, and Maria's head appears around the half-opened door. She stretches her arms into the room and lowers a tray down onto the floor, never taking her eyes off me the whole time she's doing so. She looks nervous, wary, as if I'm going to attack her at any moment.

'Maria, what's going on?' I ask, trying to keep my voice normal, although every part of me wants to scream at her.

She doesn't answer, already retreating from the room.

'Maria! Please, help me, tell me what's happening!'

The door closes, the sound of the key being turned.

She's gone.

Briefly, I think of the razor blade in the

bathroom, the scissors in my pocket: the damage I could do to someone with them. Am I capable of actually inflicting harm on another human being? I imagine myself slicing Maria's face with the blade; the blood gushing from the open wound, her screaming, my pushing her aside and escaping from this room.

I think about it for a moment and I know that I absolutely could do it. Will do it, if I need to. She's left food and water again; another sandwich and a banana. She's also left me something else that she wasn't aware of; the time. When she stretched her arm out, I saw her watch. It's twelve-thirty. I don't know if it helps to know the time because I have no way of measuring the passing of it.

I go over and pick up the tray and return to the bed and eat the sandwich. It has ham inside but could easily be cheese because I can't taste anything; I could be eating cardboard. Chewing slowly, I eat it all and then consume the banana, taking swigs of water between. Is this it for the day? One sandwich? Or will there be more? Yesterday it was one sandwich only. At this rate, the weight will drop off me.

If I'm alive long enough.

A noise at the door makes me sit up straighter. I push the tray to the end of the bed, out of the way. My heart pounds in fear as the door opens and Evan strides into the room. He stands in front of me, legs akimbo, only a few feet away. He's confident, not nervous, not like Maria. I can't tear my eyes from the door. It's still open. If only I had two good legs, I could make a run for it.

'Ah, I see you've eaten your lunch. I trust it was acceptable,' he says, his voice infuriatingly polite, as if I were a guest rather than a prisoner.

'Where's Joe?'

'Safe,' he replies. 'For now.'

My stomach tightens and I will myself not to cry. 'What have you done to him?'

He smiles. 'Too many questions, Beth. His fate is in your hands. You can keep him alive if you do as I say.'

His pale eyes lock onto mine, unblinking. Fear had me in its grip when he entered, but now, anger rises, burning away the terror.

Spit it out, you bastard.

'What do you want?'

He tilts his head slightly, as if considering the question for the first time. 'What do I want?' he muses. 'What I want, Beth, or should I say, *Lizzi*, is for you to send a message to your father telling him I'll release you and Joe as soon as he's paid me two million pounds.'

CHAPTER NINE

Money.

Of course. Isn't it always about money?

Evan smiles at me and the urge to rip the nail scissors from my pocket and stab him in the eye with them is so strong that I have to clench my fingers into fists to stop myself. To even try would be pointless because he would easily overpower me, but nevertheless, the desire to do it is almost overwhelming. Could I do it, inflict such violence on another human being? I imagine his eye exploding into pieces as I plunge the scissors in. A vision of blood and gore unreels itself across my brain in horrific colour and instead of feeling sick at the thought of it, I know that given the chance, I absolutely would do it.

I'm shocked at my capacity for violence.

'You will make a video which we will send to your father and once I receive my money, I'll let you both go,' he says the words with a hint of a smile on his face and I have to look away from him to stop myself from attacking him.

I don't believe for one minute that he'll let us go.

Both Joe and I have seen Evan and Mick's faces.

No way will he take the risk of me and Joe identifying them to the police. They'll ensure that there are no loose ends. They'll kill us both.

'And what if I won't do it?' I ask.

He laughs, strolls to the window and looks out, studying the view. He's relaxed, sure of himself, confident that I won't attack him.

'Then Joe will die', he says, turning to face me. 'We will film you saying exactly what I tell you to say or I'll kill Joe. That is your choice. If you want him to live, you'll do as I ask.'

Ask. What a joke; it's not as if I have a choice.

'I'll do it, but please, let me see Joe.'

'When your father has paid the ransom, you can see him.'

'Where is he? Where have you taken him? Why can't we be together?'

'He's alive. For now, that's all you need to know,' Evan says. 'Do as you're told and he'll stay that way.'

With that, he walks out of the room, closes the door, and I hear the door being locked.

Will I ever see Joe again?

Sudden, bitter anger threatens to overwhelm me, and I want to scream. Cold, silent rage at Evan, but also anger at Joe. If Joe hadn't drunk so much and bragged about my dad, Evan would have had no clue who my dad was and wouldn't be holding us to ransom. We'd be leaving today and going home and our lives would continue as normal.

Why the hell did this have to happen?

It never crossed my mind it would be something to do with Dad but I should have known, because in my old life when people knew who I was, it was always about money, every time. But life has been so different since Joe and I have been together that I've become accustomed to living a normal life, doing normal things, having normal friends. Yes, we have a lovely house that's paid for but I never talk about his wealth to anyone. I left that life behind. If we discuss our families with our friends, it's in general terms and money isn't mentioned. Joe's family are poor, but he doesn't advertise that fact either, because it's not relevant to who we are. Our friends assume Joe and I are in a similar situation to them and have a big mortgage to pay because we've never told them differently. We both work, even though I haven't since I broke my leg because it's not possible to temp at the moment. No one knows our financial situation in the same way that we don't know anyone else's. Personal finances aren't a subject that we discuss with friends. Which suits me just fine, because I don't want to be seen as a trust fund baby, a princess, a spoiled brat.

What are the odds of our car breaking down in the vicinity of a criminal who sees an opportunity to make easy money out of us?

A million to one, surely, but somehow it's happened. If only we hadn't come away on this stupid spa weekend, it would never have happened. We'd be safe at home together instead of living this nightmare that's going to end in our deaths.

Do something about it.

Look at the situation, Beth, see what you can make of it because there must be something you can do. There is always some action you can take, that's what Dad says.

Do nothing and die.

I have to find an angle, a way to get out of here, so stop crying and being angry and *think,* Beth.

Taking several deep breaths, I wipe my tears away. Okay. I'm being held for ransom, but on the upside, at least I know now that the aim is not to torture me or make me a sex slave. I hope. Although Evan could do that too, just for fun, because there's nothing to stop him and he's going to kill me, anyway.

Don't think about that; it won't help.

I know Dad will pay the ransom immediately. He won't go to the police because he won't risk anything happening to me. If there's one thing I'm absolutely certain of in this world, it's Dad's love for me. We may not always agree on everything, but I've never for one moment doubted his love. The real problem is that as soon as Evan has the money, Joe and I will be of no further use to him and he'll kill us.

And there's nothing I can do about it.

He may have already killed Joe, because what reason is there to keep him alive? I gasp at the thought of never seeing Joe again, at the thought of what they might have done to him.

It's unbearable.

Stop. Don't think about it because it won't help you get out of here.

So what can I do? Try to persuade Evan not to kill me? I don't think that would work because he's not stupid. If I promised never to tell the police anything about him, he'd know that the minute I'm free, I'll be helping them all I can.

What if I try to delay the inevitable, play for time? Make myself stronger, prepare myself so I have a better chance of escaping and getting help? I could try to get out of this room, because there must be a way, I just haven't found it yet.

I get up from the bed, go to the door, put my ear against the wood and listen. Silence. For now, I'm alone. I walk over to the door to the bathroom and resume my walking up and down the room.

And as I walk, I'm thinking, because there must be a way out of here.

◆ ◆ ◆

'Carry her,' Evan snaps. 'It'll be quicker.'

Evan and Mick are in my room. It feels as if several hours have passed since Evan was here earlier and I've spent most of that time walking, interspersed with brief rests. I can walk unaided now but it's tiring and much easier with at least one crutch, but at least I know I can do it if I need to.

'Where are you taking me?' I ask, my voice feeble and pathetic.

Evan doesn't speak, but strides impatiently out of the room. Mick looms over me, scoops me up off the bed and we follow him. He races down the landing, carrying me as if I were a rag doll. I'm totally powerless, and the speed at which he's walking and the sheer drop from the balustrade into the hallway as he powers along feels precarious. He could toss me over the side if he chose to. A vision of my body hitting the marble stoned hallway, my skull cracking open, flashes across my brain, making me feel nauseous. We're soon flying down the stairs, two at a time, and following Evan into the library. Once inside, Mick puts me down onto my feet so suddenly that I overbalance and he has to catch my arm to stop me from falling.

'For Christ's sake, put her in the chair,' Evan snaps. 'She can't stand up. She's got a broken leg, remember?'

Mick stands perfectly still for a moment before dragging me to the chair placed in the centre of the room and roughly forcing me in it. The tops of my arms feel bruised where his fingers have bitten into the flesh. I rub at them and wince. Mick steps towards Evan, muttering under his breath and although I don't catch the words, it's apparent from Mick's body language that he's angry. After a few moments of hissing at one other underneath their breath, Mick steps away from Evan.

'Just remember to stop telling me what to fucking do and we'll be good,' Mick snaps, his voice loud. Evan's normally pale skin is flushed as he glares at Mick, but he doesn't reply.

So Evan isn't really in charge. It was all an act, a lie. Of course it was; these are criminals, not a master and his servant. But why are they here? And what's Maria's role in all of this? Maybe Mick holds the advantage – he's bigger, stronger, more imposing. Or is Evan the brains behind the two of them? I steal a glance at them; they've put some distance between each other now, both deliberately avoiding eye contact, the tension between them almost tangible.

I look around the room; sheets have been hung over the shelves full of books behind me, covering them entirely. This must be so the background in the video will give no clue to where I am.

'Where's Joe?' I ask, loudly.

'Shut up,' Evan says. He walks over to stand in front of me.

'I want to see him. Please.'

He suddenly lurches towards me, leans down and pushes his face close to mine.

'Shut. Up. You talk when I say you can,' he hisses, spittle flying from his mouth. He's on edge, angry even, not his usual calm self at all. I cower in the chair and it tips backwards and I think I'm going to crash to the floor, but Evan grabs hold of the arms and pulls me upright again. He stares at me for a moment and then stalks away to Mick, who is watching us.

'You do the filming, yeah?' he says to Mick. I notice his accent has slipped; he sounds less well-spoken than normal and I detect the hint of a London accent.

Mick nods, taking a mobile phone out of his pocket.

'Read this.' Evan comes closer and holds a sheet of paper in front of me.

Mick holds up his phone, pointing it at me, excluding Evan from the shot. I read the words on the sheet of paper that Evan is holding.

I'm still alive.

If you want me to stay that way you have to pay them the money.

Two million pounds and they let me live.

No police. Contact the police and I will die.

They will know.

They will be in touch.

My voice is wobbly. There's no way to give Dad any hint of where I am. Give him any clues. Even if there were, I don't actually know where I am.

'Too quiet,' Evan barks. 'Read it again. Louder.'

I repeat them.

'Again. Louder.'

We continue in this way until the words become meaningless and my voice robotic. Perhaps that was the intention. Abruptly, Evan turns and walks over to Mick to study the phone footage, the two of them speaking quietly so I can't hear. Moments later, Mick strides towards me, plucks me from the chair as if I were weightless, and carries me out into the hallway and up the stairs, Evan following in our wake. I see Maria standing in the doorway to the lounge as we pass by. Her face is white, her expression pinched, and she looks quickly away when I look at her. What's her part in this? I'm guessing she's not the maid or the housekeeper, as I thought. Maybe she's Evan or Mick's girlfriend.

Could she be the weak link?

Possibly. She's a woman. Perhaps I could appeal to her better nature.

As I'm carried up the stairs, I implore them both to let me see Joe, my pleas turning to begging when I'm met with stony silence.

'Maria will bring you food.' These are Evan's only words as he and Mick leave after I've been put on the bed. They go quickly, slamming and locking the door behind them, and are long gone by the time I get up from the bed. I bang on the door, calling to them to please let me see Joe, but am met with silence. I give up quickly, because I'm wasting my energy by calling out to emptiness. Evan said Maria will bring me food. Two meals in one day? I wonder why they're bothering to feed me when they could easily starve me, as they're going to kill me, anyway.

It's beginning to get dark outside already, and I

clamber out of bed and go over to the window and stare down at the driveway. All the snow has gone now, melted away to be replaced by drizzly rain; the sky hanging low and grey with cloud. The glass in the windows has that strange luminescence that old glass has, almost a shimmer, a ripple. Not precision flat like the double-glazed glass we have now because this is an old house and the windows are original. Taking hold of one crutch and using the other to steady myself, I heft the crutch in my hand and tap the handle grip on the glass. The grip is made of hard, shiny plastic, not soft rubber like the foot. It has to be tough because with a hand on each grip; it has to take all of my weight and more. These crutches are made to take the weight of an adult male. Making sure that I'm stable, I grip hold of the crutch and swing it as hard as I can at the windowpane. The glass cracks, a line growing from the top to the bottom of the window frame. Taking aim, I hit it again near the crack and the blow shatters the glass with a deafening noise like a gunshot. Broken glass scatters across the carpet, while jagged shards cling stubbornly to the window frame. Knowing that at any moment they'll come bursting into the room, I snap off a large piece of the glass that's still hanging in the frame. I look at it for a moment.

Here goes.

Taking a deep breath, I clench my jaw tightly and drag the jagged edge hard across the inside of my wrist. The pain is raw and burning and I watch as my skin splits open and blood spills out in a red rush. Dizzy now, with the world tilting, I pass the glass to my other hand, my fingers shaking and slippery with blood. I hold the glass against the skin but my brain refuses to make it move.

Do it now Beth, because they'll be here any minute.

I push down hard with my fingers, crying out as I slice deep into the skin, blood bubbling from the wound.

It's done.

CHAPTER TEN

So much blood.

My trousers are splattered with it, the bright red stark against the pale blue denim. Strangely, I feel no pain now. Carefully lowering myself onto the floor, I lie down and close my eyes.

Seconds later, the door flies open, hitting the wall with a force that rattles through the room.

'For fuck's sake!' Evan, his London accent stronger now, sounds panicked as he thunders across the room towards me.

'Oh my God, is she dead?' Maria now. She sounds terrified. Maybe she can't stand the sight of blood. The light through my closed eyelids darkens and I sense Evan is close to me. His fingers, cold and firm, clamp around my wrists.

'Get a towel or something,' Evan snaps.

A moment later, his grip loosens, and I feel soft, damp fabric being wrapped tightly around each wrist. Bathroom towels, I think. Pressure joins the softness, but this time I think it's Maria, because her touch is gentler, and weirdly makes me feel secure. I can smell her perfume.

'We need to get her to the hospital,' Maria says. 'She could die.'

'She won't die.' It's Mick now. It sounds as if he's over by the door. 'Not if you keep the pressure on her wrists.'

'You took your time,' Evan snaps. 'Where the hell were you?'

'I was busy with the dogs. Someone has to feed them.' Mick sounds annoyed and again, I sense animosity between them.

'I can't keep the pressure up forever,' Maria says. 'The wounds need stitching. We should get her to a doctor.'

'Shut up.' It's Evan. 'No doctors.'

'What if she dies?' Maria again.

'She won't die.' Evan snaps. 'We'll put tape on the cuts and bandage them tightly. It's not gushing out, is it? No way is she going to bleed out. Let's get her on the bed. Mick?'

Strong arms slide under my shoulders and knees. I force my body to go limp, feigning unconsciousness. As I'm lifted, my head tilts back, my limbs slack. Maria keeps hold of my wrists while Mick carries me, then drops me onto the bed with a careless thud, wrenching my arms out of Maria's grasp.

'Be careful!' Evan snaps.

The mattress shifts as Maria climbs on to the bed and takes hold of my wrists again.

'I'll go and look for a first aid box or something,' Evan says. 'There must be one somewhere.'

'What if she dies?' Maria repeats, her voice thin with fear. 'What will we do then? We can't let her die.'

'Shut the fuck up,' Evan hisses. 'She's not going to die. Get a grip. You stay here, Mick, while I go and find some bandages and don't ease off on the pressure, Maria.'

'Don't tell me what to do,' Mick says, his voice low.

'Fine. Then you decide.'

Footsteps, the creak of the door. I think Mick just left.

'She looks so pale,' Maria murmurs.

'She'll be fine.' Evan reassures her, his tone softening.

'This wasn't supposed to happen,' she whispers, her voice barely audible.

'Ssh. Watch what you say.'

Silence. Are they mouthing words to each other, having a conversation? I think they are. The temptation to open my eyes is strong, but I resist. If I pretend to be unconscious, I might find out more.

'Here.' Mick is back. 'There should be something in here.'

There are sounds of a box being opened and rummaged around in.

'This should do it. It's for taping wounds closed.' Maria's voice. The towel is unwrapped from my left wrist, the one with the deepest cuts. I wince and open my eyes as Maria wipes my skin with an alcohol wipe. It stings.

'You stupid bitch,' Evan says, making eye contact with me. 'What did you do that for?'

I don't answer and close my eyes to shut out the icy rage in Evan's eyes, lying still as Maria stretches tape over the wound, dabbing the blood away as she does so. Once she's taped it, she wraps a bandage tightly around it, over and over again, and then repeats the process on the other wrist.

'Get something to board the window up,' Evan says to Mick.

'Let her freeze,' Mick replies. 'Teach her to go around smashing stuff up.'

Evan mutters something, but I don't catch what he says. Maria finishes bandaging the other wrist and the mattress moves as she gets off the bed.

'Open your eyes.' Evan is close, his breath on my face.

I open my eyes.

'What was the point of that?' he demands.

'I can't live without Joe.'

He sighs. 'You don't have to live without him. As soon as the ransom's paid, we'll let you both go.'

'How do I know you won't kill us both?'

'You'll just have to trust me on that, won't you?'

'I don't think you'll let us go. You've killed Joe already, haven't you? That's why he's not here. He's dead.'

'He's alive.'

'No, he's dead. I can feel it. I know it. I want to die, too.'

'He's not dead, for fuck's sake.'

'I don't believe you.'

'Let her see him,' Mick says.

'NO!' Evan shouts. 'She doesn't tell us what to do.'

'I'll do it again,' I say. 'And next time I'll make sure it works and I die.'

'We could let her see him,' Mick repeats. 'Just for a minute.'

'She won't kill herself. She's not capable,' Evan says.

'A dead hostage isn't much good to you, is it?' I look at Mick.

'We'll show you he's alive,' Mick says.

'So you've decided, have you?' Evan demands, glaring at Mick. 'It's up to you, is it?'

'Thank you, Mick,' I say.

'You fucking idiot,' Evan bursts out. 'She wasn't in any danger of dying. Those cuts are superficial and look, they've stopped bleeding now. The silly bitch didn't even know what she was doing.'

Oh, I knew, Evan, I knew exactly what I was doing.

And it worked.

◆ ◆ ◆

Mick hammers a nail into the board covering the window and stands back to admire his handiwork.

I watch from the bed, my face expressionless, one thought only on my mind.

I'm going to see Joe.

Joe's alive and they're letting me see him. How long will I have to wait? I'm desperate to get to him, to see that he's okay.

Mick picks up the battered toolbox from the floor and strides past me to the door.

'When can I see Joe?' He's leaving and I need to know.

He stops, studies me for a moment. Maria is standing by the door. She's been watching me while Mick boarded the window, but I haven't moved from where he put me on the bed.

'If you do as you're told, soon.'

'Thank you.' I make myself sound grateful. Maria's eyes flicker from Mick and then back to me. Evan isn't here; he and Mick both left the room earlier, locking me and Maria inside. Their shouting was so loud from downstairs that we could hear them arguing and when Mick came back, his face was flushed and he stormed into the room and set about nailing the wood over the window without speaking a word to Maria.

'Get those,' he snaps the words at Maria and she picks up my crutches from the floor and follows him out of the room, locking the door behind her.

I wish they hadn't taken them away, but I'm not surprised that they have. They'll know I used them to break the window and won't want me doing it again on the other one. I get up from the bed and make my way over to the window. It's slower without the crutches, but the more I move, the stronger I'll get. Outside, the night is pitch black, but I leave the curtain open on the unbroken window because I need to see where they bring Joe from.

The boarding over the shattered window is makeshift, the wood clearly repurposed from a packing crate. Reaching up, I grip one slat, testing its strength. It's thin, weak. Mick hammered nails into the window frame to hold it in place, but it's flimsy. Gaps between the slats let in cold air, and along the top, an opening of a few inches leaves part of the window exposed. The gap also means I'll be able to hear if a vehicle pulls up outside, so I'll know when they're bringing Joe.

Unless he's already in the house.

I saw them take him away, but they could have brought him back without me knowing. He could be in another room because this is a big house. Looking down at the carpet, the light catches tiny pieces of glass that Maria missed when she was clearing up. Blood is spattered on the wallpaper and the carpet. A little blood goes a long way and made what I'd done look far worse than it was.

I had no intention of killing myself.

Evan was right when he said they were surface wounds, but on first sight of me with blood everywhere, they all panicked and assumed it was much worse than it was.

I had to do something; take some sort of action. I

hoped they'd let me see Joe, which, thanks to Mick, worked, but I also did it because I couldn't just sit here and wait to die.

I have the feeling that Maria is uncomfortable with what's going on and isn't happy about it. Does she not agree with what Evan and Mick are doing?

Crossing to the bed, I climb onto the blood spattered sheets, prop myself up on the pillows and think back over what I've learned.

Evan and Mick are on edge with each other, each thinking they're the boss of the other. There's definite animosity between them. Whose house is this? I can't believe it belongs to Evan. Maybe they're renting it, or moved in while the owner is away. Or worse – maybe they've murdered the owner, the occupants. Or are the owners being held somewhere, like Joe? Because they must be pretty sure that whoever lives in this is house isn't going to turn up and catch them here.

Anything is possible.

When we arrived here, Mick told us he worked here, but does he, because he clearly doesn't see Evan as his boss? Did they come up with the ransom demand after learning who my father was, or did they somehow expect that Joe and I would break down nearby?

How could that even be possible?

Or was it just bad luck? We broke down in the middle of nowhere, and a group of criminals saw an opportunity to cash in?

Neither possibility makes sense.

Is Maria Evan's girlfriend? Possibly, and if not, at the very least, they're friendlier with each other than they are with Mick. Maybe they knew each other before they met Mick.

But again, how can this be planned? It doesn't make sense.

They want me alive, for now, because they might need me to do another video for proof of life. Logic tells me they won't release me once they have the money. I've seen their faces and can identify all of them, and this house, and so can Joe.

They'd be stupid to let us go.

Maybe only Evan knows that we'll be disposed of; perhaps Mick and Maria think we'll be released. They may be up for kidnap, but murder is a different matter.

All pure conjecture on my part and would knowing their plans help me? I don't know. What I do know is that it won't take long for Dad to pay the ransom because he won't involve the police. He won't do anything that will risk harming me. He'll pay anything to get me back.

Which means Joe and I don't have long before keeping us alive is no longer necessary.

The sound of Mick's truck pulling up outside gets me off the bed and over to the window, surprising myself with how quickly I can move without my crutches.

They've bought Joe.

Voices. Someone is outside the bedroom door.

I'm torn; I'm desperate to stay by the window

and see if Joe's okay, but if they open the bedroom door and see me, they'll know I can walk and I don't want them to have that knowledge. The more disabled they think I am, the better. Taking one last glance at the driveway, I see the truck door opening, but I tear myself away and hobble to the bed as quickly as possible, lying down as if I haven't moved since they left. My heart races at the thought of seeing Joe and I silently pray that he's okay, that they haven't beaten him again. The terror in his eyes when I last saw him is imprinted on my brain and I push the memory away, unable to cope if I think about what they might do to him.

Evan comes in first, followed by Maria.

'Get up,' Evan barks at me.

'Can I see Joe?'

'Stop talking and get up.'

'I can't walk without my crutches.' He looks confused for a moment.

'Mick said to take them,' Maria says. 'So she couldn't use them to break another window. They're downstairs.'

Evan frowns, looking through the open doorway. Is Mick out there?

'Pick her up, can you, Mick?' Evan says. 'She can't walk.' He's asking him, not ordering him. Maybe that's a result of the shouting I overheard earlier.

Mick comes in, lifts me off the bed and waits while Evan and Maria go out of the room. We follow them out onto the landing and down the stairs. Which room is Joe in?

Once downstairs, I expect Mick to carry me into the library or the lounge, but he doesn't, instead we go to the front door and follow Evan outside and head towards the truck. Evan pulls open the passenger door, and Mick climbs the steps and shoves me into the front seat, roughly pushing me along. Once I'm in, he gets out and Evan climbs in next to me, hurls my crutches onto the floor and buckles himself in.

And then I realise they haven't bought Joe to see me.

They're taking me to him.

CHAPTER ELEVEN

It's dark as we speed along the roads. They're the same roads that Joe and I drove along on Saturday.

It seems like a hundred years ago, not the day before yesterday.

The occasional car passes us in the opposite direction, but mostly it's quiet, with little traffic. Evan and Mick don't speak at all and I remain silent, gripping the edge of the seat to stop myself from sliding into Evan or Mick as we drive around bends. The thought of touching either of them is repellent, as is the closeness of Mick when he carries me.

My crutches are rolling around in the footwell, and I trap them with my feet to still them. They must be going to allow me to walk, otherwise they wouldn't have brought them.

Since we left the house, I've been counting in my head to gauge how long we've been travelling. When the tree-lined road changes to a wider road with houses scattered alongside, I estimate we've been travelling for around fifteen minutes. Scattered houses soon turn into a housing estate and I realise that this isn't a village, but a town. It's lighter now, because streetlights have appeared and we're travelling on a dual carriageway. We suddenly veer off onto a slip road and enter a sprawling housing estate. I scan for road signs to see where we are, but it's hopeless; Mick is driving far too fast to read them.

'Slow down. We don't want a speeding ticket,' Evan snaps.

Mick doesn't reply, but stamps his foot on the brake and we all lurch forward, straining against our seatbelts as the truck suddenly slows. Evan curses under his breath and I glance out of the corner of my eye at Mick. He's grinning. We drive onwards through the housing estate, weaving through smaller roads and the houses thin out again. Disappointment hits me; we're on the outskirts of the estate now, heading out of town, away from the centre. If we'd stopped there, where there were other people around, there would be the potential for getting help, the possibility of escape.

A few minutes later, we turn into what appears to be a trading estate; massive buildings, sprawling warehouses with flat roofs, and rows of low, square units, all shuttered and silent. The place is deserted. We pull up outside a warehouse and wait, the engine idling, as a large roller door slowly rises. Mick drives us inside.

Mick and Evan clamber down from the cab, and I unclip my seatbelt and shuffle along the seat. Mick grabs me, hauling me roughly from the cab and setting me on my feet. Pulling the crutches from the cab, he thrusts them towards me. A loud mechanical clang echoes through the space as the roller door slams shut behind us.

'Come on.' Evan strides off, using his phone torch to light the way in the inky blackness. Mick waits while I position the crutches underneath my armpits and follow slowly behind.

'Hurry up,' he snaps.

'I'm going as fast as I can,' I lie.

I concentrate on walking through the dimness, the feel of the concrete hard beneath my feet. It's echoey and vast in here, as if we're in an empty space. It may be, but I can see only as far as Evan's phone torch allows. Either side of us is in complete darkness. The air is chilly and smells of damp. Sudden light floods from a doorway ahead of us, illuminating the huge space we're in. It's a warehouse or some sort of workshop. The light is coming from the open door of a portable cabin. There's a man standing in the entrance, but I can't make out his features and as we draw nearer, he silently slips away into the darkness, disappearing toward what I assume is another doorway.

So it's not only Ethan and Mick, there are others involved. Fear grips my insides. This is so much worse than I thought. They're never, ever, going to let me and Joe go free.

When I get to the doorway, Mick puts a hand on my arm and holds me back while Evan goes inside, leaving the door ajar. The edge of a wooden desk is visible through the gap, confirming my guess that it's used as an office. After a moment Evan comes back out, nods at Mick and then I feel Mick's hand on my back, hustling me forward, scarcely giving me time to find my feet.

I stumble into the office, only my crutches keeping me upright and preventing me from falling, and my leg screams in pain. I keep my eyes on the floor to see where I'm going and when I look up, I see Joe sitting on a chair in the corner of the room. There's a gag tied around his mouth and his arms are pulled behind his back. He's tied to the chair and his coat is ripped, his face battered and bruised, his eyes wide open in shock as he stares back at me.

'Joe!' I gasp.

'Shut up!' Evan snaps. 'No talking! Now you've seen him, we're leaving.'

'No! Just let me talk to him for a minute. Please.'

'No. He's alive. That's all you need to know.'

'Please. I just want to hear his voice.'

'For fuck's sake.' Mick strides over to Joe, leans down and mutters something to him before yanking the gag down over his chin. Joe coughs, spittle flying from his mouth.

'Are you okay Joe?' I ask.

'Why are you covered in blood?' Joe asks, sounding angry. With renewed shock, I see that his front tooth is chipped, the corner of it missing.

'What have these bastards done to you?' he demands.

'I'm fine, it's nothing,' I say, stumbling over the words, wishing that I'd changed my clothes to stop him from worrying about all the blood. 'They've done nothing to me. It was just a cut, that's all. A stupid accident that looks much worse than it is. But you....'

Joe suddenly kicks out at Mick with his feet, and even though his legs are bound with rope, his boots connect heavily with Mick's shins. Mick staggers, just managing to stop himself from falling over. When he recovers his balance his face is full of rage and he swings one enormous arm around, his fingers curled into a fist, and punches Joe in the face with such force that it knocks him, and the chair, over. Lying on the floor on his side, Joe cannot move out of the way as Mick steps closer, swings his leg back and takes aim at his face.

'Please! No! Stop!' I scream. 'You'll kill him!'

Mick hesitates for the briefest moment and then, suddenly, out of nowhere, Evan is there, standing in front of Joe, preventing Mick from kicking him. Evan and Mick glare at each other in tense silence before Mick abruptly spins around and storms across the room and out of the door, nearly knocking me over as he passes me. Evan watches him go before gripping the back of Joe's chair and pulling him upright.

Blood is flowing from Joe's mouth, and he looks dazed. I walk towards him.

'Stay there.' Evan blocks my way.

'Let me help him, please, he's hurt.'

'He's fine. It's his own fault. We're leaving now.'

'Please.'

'Out.' Evan takes hold of my arms and pushes me towards the door.

'Why can't I talk to him? Please?'

'When the ransom's paid, you can talk all you like.'

'Leave her alone, you bastard,' Joe shouts.

Evan sighs. 'Get going, before I change my mind and let Mick at him.'

'I'm sorry,' Joe shouts. 'It's all my stupid fault. If only…'

Evan lets go of me and turns around. In two strides, he's in front of Joe and yanking the gag back over his mouth.

'It's not your fault, Joe,' I shout. 'Don't ever think that.' The thought of him blaming himself for this is unbearable.

'Why can't I stay here?' I ask as Evan pushes me through the doorway. 'I could look after Joe. Why do we have to be kept apart? You'll still get your money.'

Ignoring my pleas, Evan drags me, stumbling, to

the truck, the crutches clattering along the ground as he pulls me along. When I glance behind me, the door to the office is still open and a tall, thin figure emerges from the side of the cabin and goes inside. The door closes.

How many of them are there?

'You'll have to get her in,' Evan says to Mick, who's leaning against the truck smoking a cigarette. Mick takes another drag, flicks the burning end away and wordlessly picks me up, my crutches clattering to the floor as he does so. He climbs the steps, and all but throws me into the cab. Evan climbs in after me, hurling my crutches onto the floor.

'Who's the man with Joe?' I ask.

'Shut up.'

Mick climbs in and starts the engine and once the shutters are opened, we pull out into the car park and onto the road out of the trading estate. No one speaks as we drive and I sense tension between them.

What the hell is going on and why are they keeping Joe there? How many people are involved in this? Reassured that Joe is alive, I'm now more afraid than ever because this kidnapping can't have been a chance opportunity by thieves. It didn't just happen because Evan found out who I was. Breaking down in the middle of nowhere wasn't an accident.

Someone planned this.

Someone has been watching us for weeks.

◆ ◆ ◆

'What are you doing?'

'Getting fuel,' Mick replies, pulling the truck into the access lane to Tesco's.

'Are you fucking mad? It's right next to the shop. There's too many people about.'

'Okay. We run out of fuel then.'

'You should have made sure we had some.'

'Well, I didn't, did I? So it's your choice, *boss man*. You decide whether we run out of fuel or we go get some.'

'Get fuel but not here,' Evan snaps. 'Go to the place on the dual carriageway. There'll be no one there.'

We swing onto the fuel station forecourt, driving right through the lanes to the pumps, only avoiding hitting them by the tiniest fraction. Mick is throwing this truck around like it's nothing, rage apparent in his every move.

'Slow down,' Evan says quietly.

'Fuck off,' Mick replies.

We're barrelling along the dual carriageway now, the engine roaring as we speed along. Would we survive if we had an accident? As long as it wasn't too bad, it might be the best thing that could happen. I have a seatbelt on and this truck is a monster, so we'd be more protected than if we were in a car.

'Police,' Evan shouts.

The truck slows, not suddenly this time but gradually, and I watch as a police car cruises.

'It's okay, he's not interested in us. Probably late for his dinner,' Mick sniggers.

We continue along the carriageway until we see the lights for the service station. Mick slows the truck and as we pull onto the forecourt, I scan around to see if there's anywhere I could run for help. If only we'd stopped at Tesco's; it's right next to a massive store and although the store was closed, people were working in there stacking the shelves because the lights were on. Someone would have seen me, but here, there's nothing, no one. This station is on the side of a dual carriageway with no houses nearby and the shop is closed. There's no one here to serve us because it's pay at the pump.

Mick gets out of the cab, leaving me and Evan inside. I peer through the darkness as I try to think of how I can escape. The shop is shut, but I spot a sign pointing to toilets at the rear of the building.

'I need to go to the toilet,' I say.

'You can wait,' Evan says.

'I can't.'

'You can.'

'Okay, I'll wet myself here,' I say. 'Don't say I didn't warn you.'

With a sigh, he yanks open the door, jumps down out of the cab, and drags my crutches out.

I inch along the seat, lower myself onto my good leg, and hop down the step. It's awkward and Evan has to help me with the last step.

'I'll be right behind you, so don't even think about running away.'

I walk toward the toilets, going extra slow, wincing every so often so that Evan knows how painful this is for me. He's close behind me, urging me along.

'Where's she going?' Mick is standing at the back of the truck, fuel nozzle in his hand.

'Toilet,' Evan says. 'We won't be long.'

Crossing the forecourt, I wonder what I'm doing. Am I going to make a run for it?

Sort of.

Because whilst there are no houses or people anywhere near here, there's a shop at this fuel station; a mini market. And even though it's not open because it's a Sunday night and it closes early, it will be alarmed.

If I can set the alarm off, eventually, someone will come to see why it's ringing.

The police, hopefully.

It won't work, my brain tells me, it's hopeless. I'll never outrun either of them, so why am I even trying?

Because I have to do something, I can't just wait around for them to kill me. Doing something is better than doing nothing.

We've reached the back of the building and I head towards the ladies' toilet. The door is worn and battered and as I try to open it, for a moment I think it's locked because it doesn't move. I lean into it, putting all my weight behind it and shove as hard as I can. It opens.

'Hurry up.' Evan leans up against the wall, pulling his phone from his pocket. 'Be quick or else I'll come in and drag you out.'

Ignoring him, I go inside the toilet and close the door, pushing the bolt across. A weak wall light came on as I entered and I assume its motion activated. The toilet is grim with a broken seat, the bowl filthy and spattered with disgusting brown marks. There is no toilet paper, no soap, no towel.

There is, however, a window.

It's shoulder height; the lock is broken, and the window is swinging free. I could fit through it easily and make my escape across the fields behind the service station.

That's if I could climb up there, but I can't. Or maybe I could, but it would take me so long that by the time I'd got out of the window, Evan would be waiting on the other side for me.

Give up Beth, accept your fate.

No. There must be something I can do.

I can't outrun Evan. It's impossible, but what if I could make him think that I'd escaped? Draw him away so I could get out of here to get to the shop? If I swing one of my crutches at the door and crack or break the glass, maybe it would trigger the alarm.

It could work.

'Hurry up in there!' Evan shouts from outside, banging on the door.

'Okay!' I shout.

I press the handle to flush the toilet and, amazingly; it works. Standing to one side of the window, I reach my hand up, grab hold of the window, swing it wide open and then drop it, making a loud thud.

'Come out, now!' Evan hammers on the door. 'Or I'll break this door down.'

I stay silent and flatten myself against the wall to the side of the window, where, with luck, he won't be able to see me if he looks through the glass. The light goes out and the next moment; I hear movement outside. Evan is out there. I hear the window being lifted and I guess he's looking through it. Holding my breath, I stay completely still because the worst thing that could happen right now is for me to move and make that light come on.

He lets the window drop with a bang and I hear him shout for Mick. His voice is getting more distant, and I guess he's walking and scanning the field behind the garage to find me. It's dark and with luck it'll take a few minutes for them to realise that I haven't gone anywhere.

Time enough to get to the shop.

I move towards the door and, of course, the light comes on. There's nothing I can do about that; all I can do is hope they're not looking in this direction. As quietly as possible, I pull back the bolt, open the door, and step outside.

'Hello,' Mick says, stepping out of the darkness. 'Going somewhere?'

CHAPTER TWELVE

The atmosphere as we drive back to the house is weird, surreal. Mick seems to find it amusing that I tried to escape and thought I had a chance of outrunning them. I saw no reason to tell them what I really intended doing. It confused me though, the amusement, because I can't see anything funny about it, but I suppose I should be grateful that they haven't been violent to me the way they have to Joe.

And the only reason for that is that I'm no threat to them, plus they need to keep me alive until the ransom is paid.

When we pull up on the driveway to the house, Evan gets out of the cab so Mick can carry me and when I say that it's okay, I can walk, and lean down to pick my crutches up from the footwell, Evan snatches them away and takes them into the house with him. Mick picks me up with a grin and I'm carried again, baby-style, into the house. My crutches are lying on the floor inside the front door, and I look at them with longing as we pass by. There's no sign of Maria, and I wonder where she is. Mick carries me into my room, dropping me onto the bed from a height. There's a tray with a sandwich and a bottle of water on it, sitting on the bedside cabinet.

'Enjoy your meal,' Evan says from the doorway. 'It'll be your last one.'

I look at him and then Mick, who sniggers.

'Your father is paying the ransom tomorrow.'

So that's why they're so happy.

'Where? How is he paying it?'

'No need for you to know the details. But once we have it, it's all over for you.' Mick laughs and before I can speak, the door is closed and locked.

It's all over for me.

They're going to kill me.

◆ ◆ ◆

Is it safe yet? Will they have been asleep long enough?

If only I knew where their bedrooms were, that would help. What if one of them is sleeping in the room next door to me?

Stop it; they're not.

There's no one next door because I'd have heard them moving around, but even if they were next door, then I haven't heard them, which means they can't hear me. This is a big, old, solid house with thick walls and huge furniture to soak up any noise.

Do I risk it? It seems as if I've been lying here for hours, waiting, but it's difficult to know how much time has passed without a watch or a phone.

Get up.

I get out of bed but there's no need to get dressed because I already am – jeans, t-shirt, hoodie, boots. And the walking boot, of course, with two socks on my foot for extra warmth. Putting on my jacket, I zip it up. It's thin and doesn't offer much protection against the cold, but it's better than nothing.

Now I just have to get out of this room.

The slats covering the window are thin, so flimsy that a good tug will snap them off. That's the easy part, as long as the noise doesn't wake anyone. I'm praying that the walls are thick enough to soak up the noise. Then, the hard part will be getting down onto the ground below the window without hurting myself. Pulling the sheets from the bed, I tie the ends of them together, creating a makeshift rope. Luckily the sheets are not the fitted type and are huge. It's not much of a drop, just one storey, it'll be okay.

As long as I don't land badly.

Shut up. Get on with it.

Tying one end of the sheet to the wooden bedpost, I lay it across the floor to the window, checking that it's going to be long enough. Thankfully, it is. Going to the window, I take hold of the lowest slat with both hands and pull it sharply towards me. It snaps easily, and I repeat the motion with the next slat and the one after that until I've created a gap big enough to squeeze through. Next, I pick up the rope and throw it out of the window. As I lean out of the window, the ground seems like a long way down. The end of the rope dangles in the air, just above the ground.

It's just one storey, I remind myself. Get on with it because if the noise of breaking the slats has woken anyone, I don't have long.

Sitting on the windowsill, I lift up my bad leg, bend my knee, take hold of my leg with both hands and swing it outside so that I'm sitting astride the window. Grabbing hold of the rope I've made and holding the wall for support, I swing my other leg over and perch precariously on the window ledge.

Here goes.

Gripping the rope tightly, I pull it over my shoulder and slowly ease myself off the windowsill. The wrenching in my shoulders as I drop almost makes me let go, but I hang on, before forcing myself to release one hand to drop a bit lower. Repeating this, again, I make my way jerkily to the ground, my shoulders screaming for me to stop. Just before I touch the ground, I raise my bad leg as high as I can and put my other foot down to take my weight.

I've done it.

Hauling myself upright, shivering with both fear and cold, I walk up the driveway, my eyes gradually growing accustomed to the dimness. The crunching of the gravel sounds like gunfire to my panicked ears, and I know that if anyone looks out of the window now, it's all over.

Once I'm past the driveway and onto the grass, I turn to the left and head towards the open countryside. Taking a last look at the house, I'm relieved to see that no lights have come on and it's still in darkness. Increasing my pace, I walk as quickly as I can, keeping the dim outline of the forest in front of me as I head towards it.

Hobbling between the trees, I keep my eyes focused on the ground in front of me. With only the weak moonlight to guide me, I'm praying that I don't stumble down a pothole or trip over. My chest is burning with breathing in the freezing air and my legs are so tired, but I keep going until I can't walk any more. When I finally come to a juddering stop, my breath coming in ragged gasps, I position myself behind the trunk of a large oak, out of sight of the house. Am I far enough away to rest now? Is it safe? It makes no difference whether I am or not, because I have to stop. My bad leg is agonising and I need to rest it. Doubling over, I clamp my hands on my knees, inhale deeply and draw the freezing air into my lungs in an attempt to quell the dizziness and pounding in my head. Just a moment, that's all I need, a few seconds to catch my breath before I start moving again.

Despite the support of the walking boot, my leg feels fragile and weak, as if it might give way at any moment, as if the slightest movement would cause it to snap. It's possible; it broke before so it could break again. Weirdly, I felt no pain when I was moving; sheer terror and adrenaline drove me on, but now electric shocks are shooting from my ankle up to my knee. I try not to think about the potential damage I could have done, the ever present fear that I'll never walk normally again forcing its way into my head.

I have no choice. Besides, I won't be walking anywhere once they get the money and I'm of no further use to them.

My breathing more normal and my heartbeat no longer deafening in my ears, I wonder if it's safe to move again. I peer around the tree and look back at the way I've come. It's difficult to make out the house in the darkness, but if I squint, I think I can just see the outline of it in the distance. There are no lights on, no flashlights piercing the darkness looking for me, no shouting, no sign that anyone knows I've escaped.

No sound of the dogs.

I swallow down my fear at the thought of the huge, ferocious beasts and what they would do to me. They're not looking for me; the house looks exactly as it should in the early hours of the morning; dark and asleep, with no sign of life.

I can do this.

Unable to run, I've hobbled as fast as the three-inch-heel on the boot allows and although I've stumbled many times in the darkness, my foot hitting debris or dropping painfully into a dip in the ground, I've kept going. If I fall and hurt myself, I know that will be it. My escape attempt will be over and I won't be going anywhere. I need to tread carefully and not injure myself. Even if I wanted to, I can't keep up that pace I started out with even though it was no more than a hobbling trot, because it took everything I had. I used to be fit, but breaking my ankle and leg took that away from me so quickly. In a matter of weeks my toned leg muscles vanished to be replaced by something resembling a stick.

Stop.

My thoughts are wandering again.

Concentrate. Focus. You have to pay attention, Beth, if you want to get out of here.

They don't yet know that I've escaped; the house is asleep, and it's assumed I am, too. They have no idea what I've been planning and assume that I can barely walk, so if I'm lucky, I won't be missed until it gets light and they check my room. As far as they're concerned, I'm trapped in that room, barely able to walk.

They laughed at my attempt last night to get away.

The nearest village can't be that far from here; this is England, not America, and nowhere is very far away from anywhere else. The place we drove to last night wasn't that far but there could be somewhere nearer. Even if I have to walk until it gets light, I'll find a village or at least a house, someone who can help me and call the police. I'll find a road, and there'll be traffic when it gets light, I'm sure of it. I can flag down a car. My clothes are covered in blood so someone will take pity on me as I don't look like your average hitchhiker.

If my leg holds up.

If only I had my crutches with me because then I could move more quickly. But at least I *can* walk. Right now, there's no point in worrying about what damage I might be doing to my leg because I have no choice. Walking is my only way of escaping. Straightening up, I look up at the sky to check where the sliver of moon is. If I keep it in front of me, I'll be moving away from the house. I think. I hope. It would be so easy to walk around in circles because the trees all look the same and once I lose sight of the house, there's nothing to guide me. I have no idea where I am so all I can do is keep walking in a straight line and hope that I'm getting further away from *them*.

Limping slowly along, I marvel at how I managed to almost run when I climbed down from the bedroom because now, each time I put my foot down, pain radiates up through my leg. The cold isn't helping, either. Coming outside in this temperature was a shock. My thin jacket isn't much use and if I don't keep moving, no matter how slowly, the shivering will take over. My fingers are numb and even with my hood up, my ears are so cold they ache. I power onwards. After a while, I get into a sort of rhythm, realising that if I exhale as I put down my bad leg, it somehow makes the pain more bearable. Now and then, I stop and turn to look behind me, squinting through the darkness, each time relieved that there are no lights, no sounds. But it's unnerving; it's so dark and the rustles of animals in the undergrowth are alarming, even twigs snapping as I walk are making me jump.

Keep going.

And then, at last, the trees begin to thin and the ground flattens out, making walking easier. In the distance, I'm *almost* sure I see a faint light. Am I nearing a road or a house? Who would be driving this early in the morning?

What time is it? At a guess, it could be two or three in the morning, but I don't actually know. How long have I been walking? It could be hours, equally it could be thirty minutes, because time has ceased to have any meaning.

Moving forward, I see that there *is* a road ahead of me. Weak moonlight is shining on tarmac, the black smoothness so very different from the forest floor. Speeding up my hobbling, I ignore the pain because suddenly I'm invigorated and hopeful. So hopeful that at first, what I'm hearing doesn't register.

Dogs barking.

I stumble to a stop and listen, holding my breath to block out the sounds of my own breathing.

Definitely dogs.

Sick with fear, I know it's impossible to outrun them, even if I were fit. Those huge hounds will eat up the ground between me and them, and I only have minutes before they find me.

Unless I can get to the road.

Perhaps I'll get lucky and a car will drive by. It's a weak hope, a near impossibility that would need a miracle, but I speed up nevertheless because it's all I have. The sound of the barking is joined by the sound of my own heart pounding in my ears as I plough onwards as fast as I can. I can see the road clearly now. There are white markings in the middle and in the distance, joy of joys, the headlights of an approaching car.

Hurry, Beth, hurry.

And then I stumble as my foot catches in a dip, and unable to stop myself, I tumble headfirst onto the ground, my outstretched hands meeting earth and stone as I land painfully, my legs sprawled behind me. Dazed, I pull my head out of the dirt, clods of it sticking to my face, the taste of mud in my mouth.

Get up.

Pulling myself painfully to my knees, I look up to see the headlights drawing closer. Just a little further and the driver will see me, the car will stop and I'll be safe. If I can just get up on my feet and take a few more steps, I'll be home free.

Or I could crawl.

The barking is closer now, so close. Pulling my

arm up, I attempt to reach both my arms forward, to crawl, but the snarls and excited yelps from the dogs are so loud now that I fancy I can feel their breath on me. It's your imagination, the voice in my head screams, it's fear, that's all.

Move.

I lift my head and look behind me. Through the darkness I see the dogs bounding towards me from the trees, their excitement palpable at finding their prey. Snarling and barking, they gallop towards me and my brain is telling me to move, to run, to crawl, to *do something,* but my body refuses to obey.

I'm done, spent. I have nothing left.

I lay down on the wet earth, curl up into a ball and pray for it all to be over.

CHAPTER THIRTEEN

When I open my eyes, I'm dazzled by bright light. Squinting, I see that sunlight is streaming through the window and shining directly into my eyes. I pull the cover over my head to block it out. Last night's nightmare is still fresh in my mind; the dogs pouncing on me, their sharp teeth pulling at my clothes, their claws scrabbling at my body, the smell of their fetid breath as they attacked me.

Only it wasn't a nightmare, it was real.

Curled into the foetal position, I attempt to move my arm and wince at the pain. My whole body is stiff, rigid, as if I've been locked in this position for days. Attempting the slightest movement is excruciating. My head is pounding, as if it were being shaken, making my brain rattle around inside my skull. My mouth is parched, my eyes dry and sore. I push my tongue through my lips and it feels alien, as if it doesn't belong there. It's swollen to twice its size and as I run it along my lips, I encounter cracked and dry skin.

But incredibly, I'm alive.

Opening my eyes again, I look down at myself underneath the bedding. I need to know what damage the dogs have done to me. In the dimness I can make out that I'm still wearing the clothes I attempted to escape in. Gingerly moving my arms, I ignore the pain and pat my hands around my body, feeling for damage, for wounds. Aside from the aching in my bones, I think I'm okay. Stretching my legs straighter, my feet snag on the sheets. I still have the walking boot on one leg and my boot on the other. Although there are what look like dark patches on my clothes, I think that they're mud from when I fell, and not blood.

Did they stop the dogs from attacking me? They must have, because they would surely have ripped me to shreds otherwise. My last memory is of overwhelming terror as the dogs leaped at me but what happened then, I don't know. All I remember is endless nightmares, their details now lost, playing on an endless loop until the morning sunlight woke me.

So I'm alive.

But it's only a temporary reprieve, I know that. Today Dad will pay the ransom and then I'll be of no further use to them. Once they have the money, Joe and I will be murdered.

Is it even worth trying to get out of bed?

No, but I'll make myself do it, anyway. I need to get up, force myself into the shower, wash my hair, put on fresh clothes.

Why bother when I'm going to die, anyway?

Because there's always hope and I'll be dammed if I'm going to lie here and do nothing. I'm going down fighting and I'm not going to make it easy for them.

Throwing back the cover, I haul myself upright and swing my legs over the side of the bed all in one painful movement, with every part of me screaming to stop to ease the shooting pains that ripple through every bone. I do it quickly, despite the pain, because if I hesitate for just one moment, I'll crawl back beneath the covers and give up.

What the hell?

I take in my surroundings, the logical part of me knowing that this is my mind's way of shielding me from the reality of what will happen to me today. My brain is preventing me from having a total breakdown, from losing my grip on sanity. After all, who could stay composed knowing they're going to die and are powerless to stop it?

This is a hallucination.

Closing my eyes, I lay back down and focus on my breathing; in through my nose, out through my mouth. After several minutes I sit up again. Taking hold of the skin on the back of my hand between two fingers, I twist it several times with increasing pressure. It hurts like hell, leaving angry red marks on my skin.

I look around me. Nothing has changed.

This can't be real. *You're imagining it.*

Okay, my mind tells me, let's just go with it, see where it leads. Where's the harm?

Looking slowly around the room, I take it in; the pale blue curtains pulled back on either side of the window that match the duvet cover on the bed, the blue picked out in the upholstered seat in front of the dressing table.

My dressing table.

My bed.

My curtains.

I'm back, in mine and Joe's home.

Pushing myself up from the bed, I stand upright, testing the weight on my bad leg before walking to the window and looking outside. Joe's car is parked in the driveway in front of the garage.

Where it's always parked.

A neighbour across the road is washing his car, the black Mercedes that's his pride and joy. Jean, our elderly neighbour who lives in a bungalow at the end of the cul-de-sac, is slowly making her way home, shopping bag in hand. Every day she walks to the local shops, regular as clockwork. Her daily exercise, as she calls it. I can't help feeling impressed with my brain, not only is it trying to convince me that I'm home, it's factoring in trivial details to make it more convincing.

So where's Joe? What has my brain done with him?

My heart lurches at the thought. Could this be real? If it were a dream, wouldn't he be here, alive and well?

He would.

I go out onto the landing and down the stairs. When I get downstairs in the hallway, everything is exactly as it should be; our coats hanging on the coat rack, the welcome mat Joe and I bought back from Spain in front of the door, and the flowers I bought just a few days before we left on Saturday are on the table in the corner. They're starting to wilt now, one lone petal lying next to the vase.

Moving more quickly now, I go into the lounge. Joe's not there; the room is exactly as we left it, the faint smell of roses in the air from the diffuser on the mantelpiece. Leaving the lounge, I go back through the hallway and into the kitchen, desperate now to find Joe because I think maybe this could be real and not a dream. The elation I feel at being back home is stoppered, stuck, lodged in my throat because without Joe, it means nothing.

I have to find him.

He'll be there, in the kitchen, he will.

The disappointment as I open the door to see the room is empty is overwhelming, crushing. This is our favourite room, the place where we spend most of our time, one of us sitting at the table or lounging on the sofa whilst the other cooks. It was Joe, mostly, who took charge of the meals.

Why am I talking about him in the past tense?

What do I do now? I'm lost without him and being back here means nothing if he's not here with me. Collapsing onto the sofa, head in hands, I know I should do something, call someone, Dad, I think. My brain is racing ahead, trying to plan what to do, rationalising. Dad has paid the ransom and the kidnappers have released me, but not Joe.

What have they done with him?

I know the answer but refuse to believe it.

A bell starts to ring and I look around in confusion, wondering where it's coming from before realising it's the doorbell. The doorbell Joe jokingly used to say could wake the dead. Hauling myself off the seat, I go out into the hallway to answer the door. Whoever it is can help. They can call the police for me, set things in motion because I just don't have it in me to do anything right now. My fingers won't work at first and refuse to grasp hold of the door handle, but after several attempts, I manage to grip it. I yank the door open with force, nearly hitting myself in the face with it in the process. Once open, I stare at the person in front of me, uncomprehendingly, my brain struggling to cope with what I'm seeing.

I step forward, my arms outstretched, sure that at any moment this world I'm imagining will disappear into the ether and I'll be back, trapped in that room, waiting to die.

But it doesn't; this is real.

Joe smiles at me, his lips cracked, his front tooth chipped, his face battered and bruised.

But very much alive.

◆ ◆ ◆

We're sitting on the sofa in the lounge, Joe gulping water from a pint glass, me watching him.

'How long is it since you've had a drink?' I ask.

'Not sure, a day, maybe more, I think.' His voice is hoarse.

He drains the glass and I take it from his shaking hands.

'More?'

'In a minute.' He takes hold of my hand, squeezing it tightly. 'I just want to sit here with you for a while. Make sure this is real and I'm not dreaming.'

He feels the same as me; we clung to each other on the doorstep, only separating when Joe began to feel dizzy. He was afraid he'd fall and pull me over, so we came into the lounge still clinging onto each other, afraid to let go.

'Who brought you back?' I ask.

He shrugs. 'I don't know, I had a sack over my head and I know I was in some sort of van because I had to lie down in the back. I thought they were taking me somewhere to kill me, bury me.' His voice cracks on the last word, and I move closer and grip his hand more tightly.

'When we stopped, they opened the doors, dragged me out and told me not to turn around. Evan told me then I was getting my life back but I thought it was his idea of a sick joke. After they'd pulled the sack off and when I saw where I was, even then, I didn't turn around. I was too terrified to move and expected a bullet in my head at any moment. Even when I heard the van roar off down the street, I kept thinking they were trying to trick me, make me move so they could kill me. I don't know how I got to the front door. I must have walked, but I don't remember; one minute I was standing in the street, the next you were opening the door.'

Wrapping my arms around him, I hold him tightly. He feels cold beneath his clothes, frail, which is ridiculous as we've only been apart for what, two days, three? Joe takes hold of my arms and gently pulls me away from him so he can see my face.

'Enough about me. How did you get back here and what happened? What did they do to you?' There's fear on his face because I must look frightening to him; my clothes dirty and bloody, mud on my face, dishevelled and filthy from my failed escape.

'They didn't do anything to me. I'm okay, honestly. I was lucky, they didn't hurt me. I don't know how I got back here. All I know is that I woke up in our bed just before you arrived. I thought I was dreaming, or dead, even, because it didn't seem possible to be back here.'

'Why all the mud?' He takes hold of my hands and sees the bandages around my wrists. 'What the…'

'I had to break the window so I could escape.' I grip his hand. 'But I knew it would make so much noise that I pretended to try to commit suicide to give a reason for doing it. It's just a few scratches, that's all. I'll tell you all of it, but for now Joe, just hold me, please.'

He wraps his arms around me, and we cling to each other tightly. Will we ever get over this, ever feel safe again?

'I'm so sorry,' he murmurs into my hair.

'It's not your fault.'

'It is. If we hadn't gone away for the weekend…'

'Shush, stop it. We're back now. That's all that matters.'

When we finally release each other, Joe winces. I pull up his t-shirt to see livid bruises around his torso.

'What did they do to you?' I start to cry.

'I'm okay. It's over.'

'Is it?'

'Yes, it is.' He tries to pull me close again, but I lean away.

'We need to call the police,' I say. 'And my dad. He must be worried sick. I'll have to go to a neighbour or something because we don't have our phones.' How I wish now that we had a landline because without our mobile phones, we're lost, isolated, cut off.

'No.'

'I meant both of us. No way am I going anywhere

without you, not even to a house on this street.'

'No.'

'Joe...'

'No police, Beth. Not ever.'

'But...'

He turns to face me, gripping my hand.

'You have to promise me that you won't tell the police anything about this, ever. And you have to make your dad promise, too. I mean it Beth. Promise me, because if you don't, you'll never see me again.'

'I don't understand.'

'It's what Evan said when they left me in the street. He whispered it in my ear just before he pulled the hood off. He said that they were giving me my life back, but if I breathed one word of what happened, told one single person, then they'd come back for me. Next time, he said, they'd take me somewhere that I'd never be found.'

Joe's whole body is trembling. He's terrified, and so am I at the thought of it happening again.

'Oh God, what are we going to do?'

'We're going to pretend that it never happened, forget it, wipe it from our memories.' Joe's expression is grim.

'You think we can do that? It's not that easy to forget, is it? Every year when our wedding anniversary comes round, it's the anniversary of *that*, too.'

'I know, but we have no choice if we want to live. And your dad, too. No police. We don't tell anyone, ever.'

My life without Joe is unthinkable, but is he right? The police will surely protect us. How can we ever feel safe again, knowing that the kidnappers are still out there?

'You're right,' I say, knowing we can talk about this later. Once he's had time to think it through, he'll feel differently. For now, I'll pretend to agree, because I'm too exhausted to argue.

'Okay,' I say. 'We can do this. This weekend never happened.'

CHAPTER FOURTEEN

We're upstairs in our bedroom, taking the first steps to returning to normality; washing away the dirt, putting on fresh clothes and planning how to get hold of Dad.

He must have paid the ransom, but does he know we've been released? I don't know, but I need to let him know that I'm okay. He'll be frantic with worry. Joe says that once we're dressed, we should go to the nearest shop and buy new mobile phones so we can ring him. I know Joe's right, but I feel nervous at the thought of leaving the house.

Am I always going to feel this way?

Maybe. We stayed on the sofa for hours, talking about what had happened to us while we were apart. Joe refused to move until I'd told him everything. He was appalled at what I'd done; how

I'd pretended to slash my wrists, the risks I'd taken in attempting to escape.

He says I'm lucky to be alive.

He keeps blaming himself for what happened, saying repeatedly that if he hadn't insisted on that weekend away, it would never have happened. He can't shake his belief that he should have protected me and he's at fault. Me, I think it would have happened anyway because it was obviously planned, but Joe won't have it. He insists it's his fault. He's not said a lot about what happened to him despite my questioning, and I think that's because he's trying to protect me from the worst of it. I can see he's been badly beaten and he would only say it's because, like me, he tried to escape. Attacking one of his captors in the process ensured he suffered for his attempt.

I can't bear to think of Joe suffering.

Which is why I'm going to do my utmost to persuade him we contact the police or we're never going to be safe while they're still out there. In order to move on and live our lives, we need to be sure that those kidnappers are no longer a threat to us. Who's to say that they won't come back for more money? It would be too easy for them, because Dad paid up, so what's stopping them from doing it again?

Nothing.

I can't live with it hanging over us for the rest of our lives and when we get hold of Dad, I know he'll help me persuade Joe how important it is that we contact the police. They'll protect us. We know exactly what our captors look like and can give good descriptions. Maybe Evan and Mick are already known to the police and they have their mugshots on file because they weren't beginners, they knew what they were doing. It will mean reliving that weekend again, but they need to be caught and stopped from doing it to us or anyone else ever again.

We can't let them get away with it.

Once we're cleaned up and dressed in fresh clothes, Joe will feel differently about the police. I know he will. At the moment he's still in shock, as am I and we haven't left each other's side and even now, we're together. Joe's lying in the bath and I'm in the shower. I've locked the bathroom door, the front door, and the back door, and slid the bolts across.

As if that would stop them.

Which is why we *have* to go to the police.

The hot water is making me feel infinitely better, almost human, as if washing my hair and body can clean away the events of the last few days.

It's a start.

Rinsing the conditioner from my hair, I turn off the shower, step out onto the mat, wrap a towel around myself and sit down on the stool while I dry myself and put my underwear and walking boot on.

'So I'm thinking that I'm going to say that I slipped and fell in the snow,' Joe says from the bath.

'Makes sense,' I say, after thinking about it for a moment. 'Because if you go into work looking like that, they're going to want to know what's happened.'

'I'll work from home for the rest of the week until the worst of the bruising goes, but I can't stay off for too long or it'll look suspicious and also, we need to get back to normal.'

'They'll think we're accident prone, what with me breaking my leg and you slipping on ice.' Will we be able to keep the truth from everyone once the police are involved? Perhaps not, but that's a problem for another day.

Joe laughs. 'Yeah, I'll be the office joke for a while, but I can take it. I'll ring the dentist tomorrow and get this tooth sorted.' Suddenly serious, he watches me get to my feet.

'Are you sure you're okay? Should we get your leg checked out, make sure you haven't damaged it?'

'It's fine. Feels stronger than it did last week. We're home, we're safe, we're together, that's all that matters.' Am I okay though? I'm still in shock; at what happened and that somehow, incredibly, we're both still alive and here to tell the tale.

'We should get dressed, get moving,' Joe says. 'Go out and buy those mobile phones.'

'If the car works.'

'It's in the driveway, so unless they towed it back, it must do. If not, we'll take yours. Or call a cab.'

'How are we going to call a cab without a phone?'

'I can email from my computer.'

Of course; Joe has a computer, and I have a laptop. I never even thought of that. Suddenly, I don't feel so cut off from the world.

'I'll email Dad when we get downstairs, let him know we're okay. Tell him we're home.'

'Good idea.' Pulling the plug out, Joe clambers out of the bath. Watching him as he dries himself, I want to cry at the bruises covering his body. Why was it necessary to beat him? He was no real threat to them, he was helpless, a prisoner, like me, and outnumbered.

No way should they get away with it.

Joe unlocks the door, and as he pulls it open, my heart skips a beat. The fear that someone is on the other side is foremost in my mind. Does Joe feel like that, too? I stop myself from asking, because what good would come of it?

We go into the bedroom and by the time we're dressed; I feel a lot better.

More in control.

While I dry my hair, Joe strips the sheets from the bed and remakes it with fresh bedding. Rolling the muddy bedding into a ball, he doesn't put it in the laundry basket but places it by the bedroom door.

'I'm throwing it in the bin,' he says, seeing me looking at it. 'Bad memories. We'll get new.'

'Yes.'

'And the locks,' he says. 'We should get them all changed because they have our keys. As soon as we get new mobiles, I'm calling a locksmith. And we should change the alarm code, too.'

'We never set the alarm,' I say. We don't; we've never bothered because we've never felt the need. The alarm came with the house, but it's a perk that we've never used.

'Even so, we should change it and use it from now on.'

We should. We will. But we still need to call the police. I just need the right moment to tell him this.

'I wonder where the car keys are?' Joe asks, interrupting my thoughts.

'They could have left them in the car. If not I have the spare one in my handbag.' The minute the words are out of my mouth, I realise I had my handbag with me when we left on Friday. My purse, credit cards, bank cards, are all inside it and they have that, too. They'll all have to be cancelled. Joe had his wallet on him, too, so will have to do the same.

'We should make a list,' Joe says, reading my mind. 'Things that we need to do, but first let's go get those mobiles because we can't do anything much without a phone.'

'How are we going to pay for them? They have my purse, your wallet.' I say.

'Oh shit,' Joe says with a sigh. 'I hadn't thought

about that. We'll have to ask one of the neighbours if we can borrow their phone to call your dad.'

Gathering up the dirty bedding, he goes out onto the landing. I follow behind, but he suddenly stops in his tracks.

'What's that noise?' He stands and listens and I turn my head, trying to hear over the sudden pounding of my heart. There's definitely a noise coming from somewhere. Buzzing. Or is it ticking?

'It's a bomb,' I whisper, my voice hoarse. 'They're going to blow us up.'

Joe throws the bedding on the floor, wraps his arm around my shoulders, and ushers me back into the bedroom.

'It's not a bomb,' he says, leaning down and pulling open the drawer of my bedside cabinet. 'It's your phone.'

◆ ◆ ◆

Dad's on his way and will be here soon. There were countless missed calls on my phone when Joe took it out of the drawer. Whilst we were locked in the bathroom, Dad had been frantically trying to get hold of me. Joe's phone, which was lying next to mine, also had missed calls from him. I called Dad straight back and we didn't speak for very long, although both us of had so many questions, because Dad was impatient to get on the road to us and I didn't want him driving whilst distracted. I made him hang up by promising to tell him everything when he got here. He drives fast, always has done, and the last thing I want is him losing concentration for even a second. The kidnappers told him I'd been released but refused to say where I was, telling him only that they'd let me go.

Hearing Dad's voice made me instantly feel safer than I have at any time since I woke. Ridiculous, and also disloyal to Joe, because Dad's not even here and Joe is, but that's me and my dad. He was everything to me for so many years and now, despite being an adult, we'll always have that special closeness that comes from being a one-parent family. My mother died when I was young and truth be told, I'm not sure that I remember her.

I'm sitting in the lounge now and Joe has gone out to the car to see if it'll start. He's already rung a locksmith and arranged for them to come this afternoon. Although I wanted to go out to the car with him and not leave his side, I've made myself stay in here. Be normal. I can't stick like glue to his side for the rest of my life.

But I wish he'd hurry up and come back.

When we got downstairs, we searched the house and found our suitcase and my handbag in the utility room, dumped on the floor as if we'd put them there ourselves. Everything was still inside my handbag; purse, keys, makeup, all of it. Our clothes were in our case, along with Joe's wallet and nothing was missing, everything was all stuffed inside in a jumble.

The contents of the suitcase are in the bin now, as are the clothes we arrived home in. Do we think that by getting rid of them, we can rid ourselves of what happened?

If only it were that easy.

'The car's fine, started first time.' Joe's back, bringing cold air in with him. 'The keys were lying on the passenger seat.'

'How could they have made it break down like that?' I ask. 'How is that possible?'

'God knows.' Joe sits down next to me. 'I know nothing about cars and it's not like I can ask anyone, is it? *Hey, how do you make a car break down so you can be kidnapped*?'

'About that,' I say. 'The not telling the police. I've been thinking.'

'No police, we agreed.'

'I know, but what if they come back? They could. A locked door won't stop them.'

'They won't come back. We're safe as long as we keep our mouths shut.'

'They might decide it was easy money and do it again,' I say. 'There's nothing stopping them.'

The shrill of the doorbell interrupts us.

'That'll be Dad,' I say, getting up from the sofa. Sure enough, his black Mercedes is parked behind Joe's car, askew on the driveway as if he drove up at speed and abandoned it there. He probably did.

We hurry out into the hall and open the front door. Within seconds, I'm wrapped in Dad's arms. The familiar smell of expensive aftershave and cold air transporting me back to my childhood as he crushes me to his chest. He's a bear of a man and I barely reach his shoulders; six-five in his stocking feet, as he's fond of telling everyone.

'Thank God you're okay.'

'We're fine.' I pull away, reminding him that Joe is here, too.

'You okay, Joseph?' Dad asks Joe, sounding as if he couldn't care less whether he is.

'Yeah, I'm good, mate.'

Mate. Joseph.

Joe hates being called Joseph and if anyone else called Dad *mate*, they'd find themselves being lifted bodily off their feet whilst being asked to rephrase what they'd just said.

Pulling away from Dad, I glare at both of them.

'For God's sake, give it a rest for once, will you? Have a bloody day off.' I march into the lounge and after a moment, they follow in behind. What happened with Quinn hit both me and Dad hard; Quinn fooled Dad as much as he'd fooled me. So is it any wonder he gives Joe a hard time? He's suspicious of anyone and is just looking out for me, but one day soon, I hope, he'll realise that Joe is nothing like Quinn and they'll become the friends they should have been right from the start.

'Are you okay?' Dad asks. 'What did those bastards do to you?'

'I'm fine. They did nothing to me except keep me locked up. I thought they were going to kill me as soon as you paid the ransom and I can't believe they let me go.'

He hugs me again without speaking and I realise how hard it must have been for him, not knowing if I was alive or dead. As he slowly loosens his hold, I hear him swallow repeatedly, and I realise that he's struggling to hold back tears.

I've never seen Dad this close to crying before.

'I'd have paid the ransom sooner if they'd let me. They had me running all over the place with a suitcase full of money to make sure I wasn't being followed. Ended up in a multi-storey car park at midnight. Had to take the lift to the top floor, get out and leave the suitcase and walk down the stairs. When I was home again they still wouldn't say where you were, only that they'd released you. Are you sure they didn't hurt you? Do we need to get a doctor to check you over?'

'I've told you, they didn't do anything to me, it's Joe who took the beatings.'

Dad turns to look at Joe, who's sitting next to me.

'Sorry to hear that. Have you had yourself looked at, seen a doctor?'

'No, I'm okay. Nothing broken, just a few bruises.'

'It's more than a few bruises,' I say.

'I'll put security on you,' Dad says, ignoring what I've said. 'A couple of my men can watch over you twenty-four-seven.'

'I don't want security.'

'You need it.'

'No Dad, we don't. We're getting the locks changed and we've got an alarm.'

'You should have proper security.'

'I don't want it.'

This is an argument we've had many times before today.

'You won't even know they're there. It's what I do and I insist. I'm not leaving this house until you agree.'

'We don't need it because I'm reporting the kidnap to the police because they'll protect us,' I intended to say the words firmly, but somehow, they come out all wobbly and whiny.

Joe looks at me in shock. 'They said no police, Beth. We can't risk it. They'll come back.' He sounds terrified.

'I know what they said, Joe, and I'm sorry, but how can we trust them to stick to their word? They're criminals, they lie. What if they decide they want more money? There's nothing to stop them kidnapping me again, and I can't spend the rest of my life looking over my shoulder, waiting for it to happen. If we tell the police, they'll protect us and they'll catch them because they've left too many clues behind. We've seen their faces and with a bit of investigation, they'll be able to find the house and there'll be evidence there. I'm right, aren't I, Dad?'

Dad always takes my side, no matter what, even if I'm in the wrong. He's a thousand per cent loyal to me and although I hate ganging up on Joe like this, it's the only thing I can do; to not report this would be madness. But don't gloat too obviously, Dad, I silently pray. I would never normally side with Dad over Joe, but this is the only way we're going to be able to move forward.

'Dad?' He's stroking his chin, his expression thoughtful.

'I suppose we could go to the police,' he says slowly. 'But I think we need to think about it.'

'Why?' I demand, shocked that he's not immediately agreeing with me. 'What's there to think about?'

'Well,' he says. 'There are things to consider, one of them being that the newspapers will get hold of it. You left your old life behind and it'll stir the media up again, you know that, so you'll be splashed all over the papers again and you wanted to get away from that.'

He's right; there'll be no denying who I am or who my father is once the story breaks. My quiet life of anonymity will be over and all our friends will discover that my father is a well-known multi-millionaire.

'I know,' I say. 'And although I don't want that, we don't have any choice. The kidnappers told Joe they'll leave us alone as long as we keep quiet, but realistically, they can come back whenever they like. I'll never feel safe while they're out there.'

'Which is why you need security. I can keep you protected twenty-four hours a day for the rest of your lives. I know what I'm doing, you know.' Dad gives a wry smile. *Knowing what he's doing* is a bit of an understatement; his business empire is based on providing security for high-profile clients, big corporations, pop stars, you name it, it's a given that somewhere along the line, Dad is involved.

'I know, but we shouldn't have to live like that, should we?'

'Loads of people do,' Dad says airily. 'You're overthinking it. Don't you think we had security when you were growing up? We did; you just weren't aware of it.'

'It's too dangerous to report it,' Joe says. 'The minute we involve the police, we'll be sitting ducks.'

'How can it be dangerous?' I demand. 'It'll be the opposite of dangerous because we've seen their faces and can identify them. They may already be known to the police and with luck, they'll catch them quickly. We'll be safe and I can sleep at night without waiting for them to burst into the house and kidnap us.'

'Reporting it might be the start of a bigger problem.' Dad stares at me, his expression serious.

'I don't understand. Surely it'll be the answer to our problem?'

'Not necessarily,' Dad says. 'Those men who kidnapped you, they're at the bottom of the food chain. Someone higher up orchestrated this – someone who won't have any intention of going to prison. The men who held you are dispensable, but the minute they're arrested, you'll be in more danger, because there'll be a trial and you and Joe are the only witnesses.'

'Your dad means we'll be targets,' Joe says. 'So if we go to the police, we might as well tape bullseyes to our backs.'

CHAPTER FIFTEEN

'Are you sure you're ready?' I ask.

Joe leans forward as he slips his coat on and kisses me.

'I am, but more importantly, are you going to be okay? I can work from home if you want me to. It's not a problem.'

'No, you go, I'll be fine. Besides, I'm going out, remember? Dad is picking me up in an hour.'

'If you're sure.'

'I absolutely am. Now go, or you'll be late.'

We hug and then I practically push Joe out of the house because if he doesn't go quickly, I'll cave in and he'll end up staying home with me and I'll cancel everything that Dad has arranged for today. I know Joe is feeling nervous about returning to work, not least because he has to do a lot of lying when he gets there. We've been home for nearly a week now and although the bruises on his face have faded, they're still showing. Questions will be asked so he's pre-empted a lot of them by letting his manager and colleagues know that he had a fall in the snow, but people will expect him to chat about what happened as if it's no big deal. Luckily, the dentist fitted him in to repair his tooth and now you would never know it had even been chipped.

I'm sure he'll feel relieved once today is over.

And so will I. Today will be the first day anyone except for Joe and Dad has come into this house since we came back and I'm feeling anxious about it. Ridiculous, especially since Dad has arranged for his security team to install our new alarm system. By tonight, our home will have the best security available, installed by Dad's trusted men. They're not going to kidnap me, or harm me, but try telling my brain that. If I think about it too much, I'll freak out at the thought of strange men being in the house and cancel the whole thing.

Because we haven't reported what happened to the police.

The threat of what they would do if we did, the possibility of me and Joe being targets if it got to trial, or having to go into witness protection, stopped us. Dad insists that he can keep us safe. He protects others from far bigger threats than the one to us and has never lost a client yet.

So we have security now.

They're so discreet that Joe and I aren't even

aware of them. Dad's given us mugshots of them all so that if we do notice the same faces after a while, we can be sure that they're *protecting* us, not getting ready to abduct us. When I asked Dad if he'd be adding additional staff to shadow Joe separately now he's going back to work, my question was met with silence, which I took for a 'no'.

I'm trying not to panic about that.

Although Dad has reminded me more times than I care to remember, that I'm the one worth kidnapping, not Joe.

So it's better that I won't be here when they're fitting the new alarm. We'll have lunch at one of our favourite restaurants and spend the afternoon at Dad's house. He's assured me his team will clean up after themselves, leaving no trace of their visit.

It's been a while since just the two of us have spent time together, and I'm looking forward to it. It seems incredible that just two years ago, London was my home. My days were filled with socialising, attending events and award ceremonies with Dad, and generally doing whatever I wanted without a thought for anything but enjoying myself and having an active social life.

Back then, I had a wide circle of friends in London, but now I realise that they were more acquaintances than true friends.

I haven't stayed in touch with a single one of them.

I haven't reached out to any of them, but

equally, none of them have contacted me since I left London two years ago. When I told my friends that I intended to change my life, get a job and live under the radar, they all thought I'd gone completely mad. Ruby, my closest friend at that time, asked me if I was having some sort of breakdown, as she couldn't understand why I would want a different life to the one I had. Coming from a wealthy family herself, she didn't envy Dad's wealth but she did envy our lifestyle. Dad and I were frequently featured in the media, with our photos appearing in newspapers and sometimes even on TV, so I was living her dream of being known.

We'd been at the same school together and although we drifted apart when I went away to university, we picked up again when I came back to London. The plan was that I would start off my career working in Dad's business as an accountant and work my way up, but it never seemed to happen. Life, as they say, got in the way. Dad, being the social person he is, wanted me by his side at events, and any real work became secondary. He didn't see the need for me to work and couldn't understand why it mattered to me.

But it did.

Because although I enjoyed socialising, after a while it began to bore me. I felt there should be more to life; something meaningful, something to be proud of. I didn't want my greatest achievement to be appearing in the gossip columns simply because I wore a dress by an up-and-coming designer. People weren't interested in me; they cared only about my appearance, my clothes, and how much money Dad had. My opinion or what I thought about things was of no value and I only stayed in that life because of Quinn; he persuaded me that it was fun and what was wrong with having fun? Was it really so awful, he asked, to be seen around town with him, or was I ashamed of him because he wasn't rich like my father?

I loved him and he made me feel guilty when he said that, so I stuck with it, telling myself that Quinn would eventually tire of the socialising as I had, and then we could melt into the background and have a normal life. For Quinn, all the attention was a novelty because, despite his charm and good looks, Quinn was what Dad jokingly called a 'back office boy.' He worked for The Winters Group in the unglamorous IT department, but Dad had high hopes for him; Quinn was going places because, as well as his good looks, he was clever and knew his stuff. Dad thought very highly of him – which was a relief, since he was usually so wary of any man I got involved with.

And then I found out that Quinn was cheating on me.

Looking back, I think he had been unfaithful from the very start. Foolishly, I believed him when he told me he loved me, but the truth was, he was just using me to get into Dad's good books, to boost his own career. He was so convincing, so good at lying. Realising I had given my all to a relationship that was built on deception was unbearable. I had put his needs above my own, but in the end, he was nothing more than a player and a user. When I discovered he'd been seeing someone else, I ended things immediately. He begged me to give him another chance, but I blocked his number and cut him out of my life. I didn't want to hear his excuses, his lies. Eventually, he stopped calling and with Dad's help, I picked up the pieces of my life and moved on.

The betrayal cut even deeper because the girl he left me for was someone I considered a friend. We knew each other from the social circuit and had even posed together at a TV awards ceremony that Dad was invited to. She was beautiful, popular, and could have her pick of men, but she took mine, although he went willingly. Even knowing this, I hated her for a while instead of hating Quinn.

I missed him.

But I couldn't forgive him knowing that it would happen again and that he didn't really love me. His betrayal confirmed what I had always feared – that my wealth made it impossible for a man to see me as anything more than a ticket to the good life. How could I ever be sure someone loved me for who I was and not for my father's money?

A few months later, Quinn had already moved on to someone else. The girl he betrayed me with was bereft, according to the gossip grapevine, and although I couldn't bring myself to feel pity for her, I knew she had been used just as I had.

I've heard nothing of Quinn since then. I've left that life behind and I don't care what he's doing now. I've moved on.

So after that, I decided to have the life I wanted and although Dad did his utmost to dissuade me, I shortened my name of Elizabeth to Beth instead of Lizzi and used my mother's maiden name instead of Dad's. Once I'd dispensed with the blonde hair and heavy makeup, I was pretty much unrecognisable and when I started work at Torrington Accountancy, no one had any idea who I used to be. They still don't, and that's what I like about my new life; I'm anonymous and just like everyone else. When I look back at old photographs of myself, I barely recognise the person I used to be. I looked like a clone of all the other blonde socialites and the space I left in that world was soon filled, ten times over.

So I'd moved on, and moved out; because I needed a life of my own where I made my own decisions. Living with Dad, it was too easy to drift along and do nothing, because nothing was expected of me. I don't blame Dad; he wanted me to have an easy life because when he was young, his life was hard, particularly when Mum died and he had to bring me up on his own. But as much as I love him, I needed my own life.

The ring of the doorbell interrupts my trip down memory lane and, pushing down the sudden racing of my heart, I go to the lounge window and check to see who it is.

It's Dad, of course, because he's come to pick me up. A van is pulled up behind my car, *Winters Security* emblazoned on the side of it. Two men are talking to Dad while he points at various parts of the house.

Grabbing my coat and bag, I open the front door. Dad and the men are now walking up the drive towards me and plastering a smile on my face, I step outside to greet them.

Because the thought of being in the house with two strange men scares me to death.

◆ ◆ ◆

'Have a proper drink.'

Dad is looking at me as if I'm mad; the drinks waiter has asked what I'd like and I've asked for a sparkling water.

'What are you having?' I ask.

'Champagne, obviously, since this is the first time we've been out for lunch together since I don't know when.'

'Okay.' I snap the drink menu closed. 'I'll have the same.'

The waiter drifts away and I smile at the look on Dad's face.

'Remember you're driving,' I say.

He frowns, then grins, remembering that it's what I always used to say to him whenever we went anywhere. We both know that he won't even finish his glass, but take a few mouthfuls and then pour himself a glass of tap water from the jug that he always requests.

'You look peaky.'

'Yeah, well, it's been a bit of a week, hasn't it?'

'It has. But seriously, are you okay?'

'I am. Or at least I will be. In time.'

He reaches across the table and pats my hand.

'You're safe, you know. There's no need for you to worry because I'm making sure you're looked after.'

'I don't need looking after.' I pull my hand away and pick up the menu. 'But if I did, Joe is my husband, you know. I'm sure he'll do his best.'

Dad frowns and opens his mouth to reply, but the waiter appears at that moment, pad in hand, ready to take our order.

'You are ready, Miss Winters?' He directs his gaze at me.

'I'll have whatever he's having,' I say, nodding at Dad.

'Mr Winters?'

'I'm having steak,' Dad warns.

'That's fine.'

Because I probably won't eat it, anyway.

While Dad orders, I look around the familiar surroundings of the restaurant. We've eaten here so many times that I've lost count. The staff know us well because we used to be regulars; Dad still is. I feel a stab of disloyalty that I didn't correct the waiter's use of my name and then remind myself that it doesn't matter. Surprisingly, even though I haven't been here for ages, I feel comfortable here, as if I'm visiting an old friend. The menu is expensive but understated, the décor, old money, not new or in the slightest bit flash. This place gets booked out months ahead, although they'll always find a table for Dad even if he hasn't booked. The heavy tables are old, the wood polished to a burnished shine, the white tablecloths pristine and perfectly pressed, the napkins thick and substantial enough to cover my entire lap, not a flimsy piece of material that's neither use nor ornament. Before I moved out, Dad and I would pitch up here in our evening wear, ready to go to a ball or awards ceremony or equally, like today, come casually dressed, me in jeans and a jumper. Dad's idea of casual is leaving his tie off for the day because he wouldn't be seen dead in a pair of jeans. He says he's worked too long and hard to wear work wear as a fashion item.

'OMG! It's you, isn't it? I can't believe it – you look so different!'

Someone is standing in front of me shrieking and it takes a few moments for it to register that it's Ruby. I blink up at her and then stand up. We air kiss and embrace and then she leans back and sweeps her gaze up and down my body, her fake eyelashes so heavy that I wonder how she manages to keep her eyes open. I used to have eyelashes exactly like that, but now I see how ridiculous I must have looked I feel embarrassed for myself.

'Hi Ruby, how are you?' I ask, putting on my best smile. Why the hell did I have to see her today?

'I'm engaged!' She thrusts her left hand underneath my nose so I can admire the huge diamond on her finger, waggling her fingers with nails so ridiculously long that she's surely incapable of picking up a knife and fork.

'Congratulations!' I say. 'Who's the lucky man?'

'Jago. Imagine! Me and Jago getting together when we used to practically hate each other.' She laughs her tinkling laugh, as if it's hilarious. Jago was one of our crowd and they didn't hate each other at all. Ruby had a massive crush on him, but he wasn't interested in her and let it be known that he didn't think she was hot enough. Handsome and charming, Jago could be witheringly bitchy when he felt like it and he had extremely high standard looks-wise for girlfriends. I'm surprised they got together, because Jago definitely didn't consider Ruby girlfriend material.

'Hey, that's great! Is he here? I should go and congratulate him, too.'

'No, he's working, helping Daddy in the business.'

'Oh, he's working for your dad, is he?' This explains their engagement. I feel a sudden pity for Ruby; he's using her. Jago always had an eye on his future and Ruby's father's business is extremely lucrative.

'Yes.' Her eyes flicker and I detect a hint of

defensiveness. 'I thought I'd take the opportunity to go out with the girls whilst he's busy. He's so demanding on my time, simply wants me with him constantly. Why don't you come over and say *hello*?' She waves at a table across the restaurant and I spot Jemima, another old friend, seated next to Rachel Phillips.

The girl who Quinn cheated on me with.

'I'd love to,' I say as sweetly as I can. 'But perhaps another time. Dad and are on a bit of a schedule today, but call me and we'll catch up another time, yeah?'

I'm giving her the brush off, and Ruby gets it straight away, but I don't care; I haven't seen or heard from her for over two years and I'm not about to go and be nice to the girl who slept with my boyfriend.

'Oh, okay,' she says, her voice flat. 'Oh wow, is that a wedding ring?' Her eyes narrow at my ring finger.

'Yes, I've been married for a year now.'

'You sly old thing! You certainly kept that quiet, didn't you? I don't remember receiving my invitation.'

'It was a low-key wedding.'

'Low-key,' she says slowly, as if I've just told her I'm a mass murderer and she's struggling to understand it. 'So what's this man's name who you've kept such a secret?'

'Joe. Joe Coburn.'

'Coburn?' She taps a long nail against her lip. 'Is

he one of the Kensington Coburns?'

'No.'

Too late, I realise that I should have been nicer to Ruby because now she won't leave until she's got her own back. I should have remembered this about her. Upset her and she's vicious.

'No?' She affects a surprised look. 'So where's he from? What does he *do*?'

'He's an accountant.'

She bursts into loud tinkling laughter, putting her hand across her mouth after a moment as if to stifle it.

'Oops, sorry. I know it's a very worthy profession. Don't you have some sort of qualification in it or something?'

'I have a degree.' Unlike you Ruby, I could add, because she failed most of her GCSEs and abandoned her A levels after a few weeks.

'You probably have lots to talk about then, don't you?' She drops her voice slightly, as if sharing a confidence with me. 'It's just I never saw you marrying someone like an accountant, you know, someone boring. Not after Quinn. I mean, he was super-hot, wasn't he? He's a hard act to follow.'

'Unlike Quinn,' I snap. 'Joe doesn't cheat.'

Her eyes dart towards her table of friends and I wonder if they heard what I said. If Rachel heard.

I hope so.

'Well, I'm sure you'll be very happy together,' Ruby says. 'I mean, you've got the look now, too, haven't you? Sort of librarian chic. Oops, did I just say that out loud?' There's the annoying laugh again and with a little wave, she saunters back to her friends.

'I thought she was a friend of yours,' Dad says quietly.

I shrug.

'She used to be.'

'You were a bit off with her.'

'Was I?' I look at him in surprise.

He laughs. 'Compared to how you used to be, yes, you were. You never used to say boo to a goose when you were with all your friends, too busy trying to please everyone.'

I suppose I was.

But I'm not that person anymore.

CHAPTER SIXTEEN

When Joe arrived home after work last night, he said it had felt good to get back to work; that it made him feel as if we were living again and moving on. Being normal.

I was relieved to see Joe waiting for me when Dad brought me home. It wasn't just that I didn't want to walk into the house alone – though Dad would have come with me – but because I couldn't shake the fear that the kidnappers might come back for Joe. Dad keeps reminding me that I'm the real target, not Joe, but that doesn't exactly make me feel any safer.

I wish they liked each other more; the two men who I love most in the world. I yearn for them to get along better, but I have to accept that it will probably never happen. They're polite to each other, aside from the occasional dig and, for now, that will have to suffice. It's not Joe's fault that Dad sees him as a gold digger; aside from Quinn, every single boyfriend that I've ever had has been viewed that way and it's nothing personal. Dad has never forgiven himself for not seeing Quinn for what he was; he's always prided himself on being a good judge of character and he thinks he let me down, so now everyone is viewed with suspicion. Dad thinks he's protecting me; looking out for me, making sure that no one takes advantage of me. He doesn't understand how insulting he's being by thinking like that and no matter how much I talk to him about it; he point blank refuses to see it my way. He knows full well that when Joe and I met, Joe had no clue who I was or how much money Dad had, but he refuses to change his manner towards him.

He's never really forgiven me for marrying Joe without telling him first. Had he known, he would have tried to dissuade me, told me that I didn't need to get married, suggest we live together, told me to wait until I'd known him for longer. In other words, said anything to stop me from marrying the man I love.

Which is exactly why I didn't tell him.

In time, I hope Dad will see that Joe is with me because he loves me and isn't out for what he can get. We don't live a life of luxury; we live a normal life and both work for a living – or at least when I get a job I will. But even knowing that, for Dad to ever admit he's wrong about something, is going to take a very long time.

The sad thing is, Joe was so impressed when he first met Dad that he hung on his every word, but gradually, the constant sly put downs from Dad; calling him 'Joseph', making comments about being a 'bean counter' and the like, got to him. Calling Dad 'mate' is Joe's little way of getting back at him because Dad hates that sort of familiarity.

One day, maybe in the not too distant future, I have hope that they'll move on and become friends because surely Dad can't keep it up forever. Because Dad's the one at fault, not Joe. Dad would do anything for me but where Joe, or men are concerned, he's completely blinkered and unable to see my point of view.

Now that we're moving on with our lives and getting on with life, 'that weekend' as we refer to it, is beginning to feel like a bad dream. We try not to talk about 'that weekend' because it's done, over, and cannot be changed.

But sometimes we can't help it.

Something as innocuous as a TV programme or a newspaper article can trigger a memory and the horror of it rears its ugly head again. In time, I tell myself, the memories and fear will fade; become something from the past that we no longer speak or even think of.

I hope.

There are new locks fitted on all the doors. Dad's men upgraded the burglar alarm to a state-of-the-art new one, adding panic alarms and sensors in every room. By the time Dad brought me home last night, the only sign that his men had been working in the house were the tiny sensors in the ceilings and the panic buttons discretely hidden behind the curtains of each room. There was not a thing out of place and I was impressed all over again at how Dad runs his company.

And as we also have a constant security team watching over us, we're as safe as it's possible to be. Stop fretting over nothing, Dad tells me. It's sorted. Move on.

Do something.

I'm trying. Joe is finding it easier than me, I think. I try to hide the fact that I'm constantly checking the windows to see who's in the street, that when I'm alone in the house, I bolt all the doors. I tell myself that I'll only check the doors are bolted once, but then ten minutes later I'll give in and check again. It's early days, I remind myself and I shouldn't be too hard on myself. It's been less than two weeks since we were taken.

Time heals.

I applied for a job yesterday, not temping but a proper, full on, grown up, permanent position in a large company with good prospects. I have to think about moving forward in my career because it won't be long before I'm back to walking normally. I don't wear the boot at all now when I'm at home and walk around the house without it and I'm finding it easy, no problem at all. My calf muscle is beginning to reappear and my leg is no longer so stick-like.

And I'm going out again today.

Zari messaged me yesterday, asking how I was. She and Tom are our closest friends and we would often meet for lunch.

Before.

Joe had already told Tom the story of how he fell over in the snow while we were out walking and we tested each other with questions so that we didn't mess it up and get the story wrong. Made up a bunch of lies in other words, because telling one lie leads to many others and if we're not careful, we'll get ourselves into a tangle with it all. It's ironic that we've done nothing wrong yet are having to lie about it.

But we can't tell the truth to anyone, not one person, ever.

Zari wanted to come to the house to see me to make is easier for me, like she has done since I broke my leg and ankle, but I suggested we meet up for lunch at one of our favourite places.

Do normal things.

She offered to pick me up and although I think I could drive because my car is automatic, I'm not sure how that would work with insurance so although I was tempted to take up her offer, I said I'd get a cab and meet her there. It's what I would have done *before*. It'll be the first time of going anywhere on my own since we've been home and I am slightly nervous about that, but I need to do it, because if I don't, I'll be taking the easy way out of everything.

Besides, Dad's men are watching me, so I'll absolutely be safe. As he keeps telling me, he's been doing this for years, so we have nothing to worry about.

So I've washed and dried my hair, dressed smartly and put some make up on and I'm ready to go.

All I have to do now is go through with it.

My phone bleeps with a message to tell me that the cab is outside. Sure enough, when I look out of the lounge window, it's pulled up in front of the house. Picking up my bag and coat, I let myself out of the front door and carefully lock it before heading to the cab and climbing in the back. Just the walking boot, no crutches now, because I don't need them. I'm barely limping, either. I'm getting back to normal.

Moving on.

◆ ◆ ◆

I pay the cab driver and he zooms off down the street. There's no sign of Zari, but I know she'll be inside the restaurant, seated at the table. She doesn't do waiting around and has probably already ordered herself a glass of wine. This is our go to place when we want a girly catch up; good Italian food and a friendly ambience. Joe and Tom aren't so keen; they say the rustic wooden tables and chairs are too small for men to be comfortable in. Joe, in particular, says he feels like he's sitting in a child's classroom.

I've barely got inside the door before Zari's up out of her seat, waving at me. Jeanie, a waitress who is always here, no matter when we visit, greets me with a smile and I weave my way through the tables to our usual spot at the back.

'It's so great to see you!' Zari pulls me in, enveloping me in her usual girly cloud of perfume and hairspray. We hug for a moment before sitting down.

'You look great, no crutches either!'

'I'm getting there,' I say with a grin.

'I ordered you a glass of wine. Thought you might need it.'

Two glasses and a bottle of white wine are on the table. I'd only intended having water or a soft drink but suddenly I think that yes, I absolutely do want alcohol.

'Thank you.' I pour myself a generous measure and we chink glasses. The sip that I intended taking somehow turns into several because it just tastes so good.

'You okay?' Zari is looking at me with concern.

'I'm fine. Just thirsty.' I laugh, putting down my glass.

'You look like you've lost weight,' she says, before adding. 'Not that you needed to.'

As she says the words, I realise that I've hardly eaten since we've been back home. We have our meals but invariably, I push the food around the plate and eat very little of it. Joe's noticed and told me that I'll make myself ill, but I just don't have any appetite at the moment. I'm finding it difficult to concentrate on anything as mundane as eating.

'It's the effort of dragging this bloody boot around all the time,' I quip.

She studies me as she picks up her wine glass and the urge to tell her everything is there; to offload it all, to talk about it, to get it all out in the open and not have to lie. I know that realistically, it wouldn't help at all, but even knowing that doesn't stop me from wanting to do it.

I pick up my glass and make myself grin at her. 'Just thinking how easy it would be to glug the whole lot down because it's so nice.'

'God, I know. Us ladies who lunch, eh?' This is what Joe and Tom laughingly call us. 'When you said you didn't want picking up, I got a cab here instead so I can have a few drinks. I've put a dentist's appointment in my online diary just in case my boss decides to check up on me. Not that he ever does. Working from home definitely has its perks.'

'Do you have any jobs going at your place?' I ask, not altogether joking. Zari's company pays well and is so laid back it's almost horizontal. 'Because I'm looking for something permanent when I'm out of this boot and back to normal.'

'I can ask HR, see if there's anything doing, keep my ears open for you? Yeah?'

'That would be great, thanks.'

'How's Joe doing?' she asks. 'God, his face, poor love, he looked as if he'd gone ten rounds in the boxing ring with all those bruises.'

I pull a rueful expression. 'I know, he was lucky he never broke his nose. He just managed to turn his head at the last minute before he hit the ground. I think he would have knocked some teeth out, too.' Sending a picture of his face to our friends was Joe's idea. He said it's what we would normally do, because didn't we send a picture of my leg in plaster when I broke it? We did, but sending that jokey message after what we'd been through felt wrong to me, as if we were belittling and making light of the experience. Joe kept his mouth closed in the photograph so his chipped tooth wasn't visible because, like he said, he looked like a down and out and while he doesn't mind a joke, he has his pride.

'It's frightening how easy it is to injure yourself, as you well know,' Zari says. 'And that snow! Hard to imagine we ever had it now. Absolute bucket loads of it in a few hours and the country comes to a standstill and then a couple of days later it's all gone, as if it was never there.'

'I know. Good riddance to it, too. Roll on the summer.'

'Absolutely. How's your leg now you've ditched the crutches?'

'Getting better all the time. I'm walking around indoors without the boot and next week I'll start walking outside without it.'

Jeanie interrupts us, appearing at our table with menus. We chat with her for a while and I feel myself begin to relax. The Bistro is starting to fill up because it's a popular place, even on a weekday lunchtime. There are several office blocks nearby who supply the place with a steady stream of customers. I order lasagne, which is pretty much what I always have here because it's so good, and Zari opts for the same. As Zari pours us our second glass of wine, I resolve to try to eat at least half of the food whether I want to or not, because I can't carry on not eating. It's become a habit that I need to get rid of.

By the time our food arrives, I find myself relaxing. I'm not sure if it's the wine, Zari's company, or being in a familiar place that I have such happy memories of, but whatever it is, it feels good. I'm not going to overanalyse it, I'll just take it as a positive. Surprising myself, I manage to eat most of my lasagne and by the time we've finished our meals, the wine bottle is empty. When Zari excuses herself to go to the bathroom, I sit at the table and for the first time since that weekend, I'm truly enjoying myself and feeling confident that life will return to normal, eventually.

My phone bleeps from my handbag underneath the table and I smile to myself; that'll be Joe, checking that I'm okay and having a nice time. He encouraged me to come today, even offered to pop out of work at lunchtime to give me a lift here, as if I'm some sort of invalid. Yanking my handbag from underneath the table, I pull my phone out and look at the screen, surprised to see that it's not a message from Joe, but from a withheld number. Delete it, don't open it, don't look, my brain commands. If it's from an unknown number, that means it's marketing spam and nothing that I need or want. Nothing good will come of opening it. But my fingers disobey me, tapping on the message to open it. As I do so, I experience a sense of foreboding; this is the threat I've been waiting for since I woke up in my own bed just a week ago.

A reminder of what they'll do to us if we don't keep our mouths shut.

I stare at the screen, my new found happiness of only minutes ago, gone.

But as the words register, I see that it's not a threat at all. But the relief that floods through me as I stare at the screen is swiftly replaced by confusion.

Do you know what your husband is up to? Do you trust him? You shouldn't, you really shouldn't.

CHAPTER SEVENTEEN

The message is all I can think about. I'm replaying it in my head, and I've looked at it so many times that the words are imprinted on my brain.

By the time Zari came back from the bathroom, I'd tucked my phone into my bag and slung it back underneath the table. We ordered coffee and chatted while we drank it.

And I behaved as if I hadn't just received a text from a withheld number asking me if I trusted Joe.

Why didn't I just show Zari the text? Laugh about it together, acknowledge how ridiculous it was? Do the obvious thing and say, *Hey, look at this?* Because it had to be a crackpot who's sent a twisted joke to stir up drama and get a reaction. Or, maybe it wasn't even meant for me and was just a mistake, sent to the wrong person because

Joe's name wasn't even on it. Or maybe some lunatic sends out random messages, hoping to cause chaos for their own sick amusement. There are countless explanations for that ridiculous text, and none of them involve Joe being unfaithful.

So why didn't I just show it to Zari if it meant nothing?

Because that message sowed the tiniest seed of doubt in me and whilst I felt like that, I couldn't talk about it with Zari or make light of it.

Because what if it was real and Joe was having an affair?

I feel ashamed for even thinking it, because Joe has never given me the slightest reason to doubt him at all. Not one single thing. But even knowing that, I can't help myself. Quinn cheated on me and I know Joe is *nothing* like him at all; he's the absolute polar opposite, but the nasty voice in my head won't let it go. *Joe's a man*, it's saying, *don't all men cheat if they get the chance?*

No. He wouldn't do that to me.

Quinn did.

So what am I going to do?

The only thing possible.

Ask him. Show Joe the message when he gets home from work, get it out in the open so I can stop obsessing about it. Put a stop to an anonymous text from a stupid person getting underneath my skin. Stop being so disloyal by allowing it to make me doubt my husband.

Zari and I part ways, getting into our separate

cabs, promising to meet for lunch again soon and thankfully, she has no clue what's going through my mind. I'm glad about that because I'd hate for her to know how easily I can doubt Joe.

When I get home, I'm impatient for him to come home from work because I need to get this over with as soon as possible, so he's late, of course. I have nothing to distract me, no dinner to cook because I've already eaten and Joe will have, too. He's thoughtful like that and will have eaten in the staff restaurant, so we don't need to bother cooking tonight.

This is the man I've allowed a spiteful, anonymous message to cause me to doubt.

I'm disgusted with myself, but even feeling like that, I'm unable to let it go and crave Joe's reassurance that he loves me, and me only. Because I can't sit still, I walk around the lounge without my boot, but this triggers memories of pacing in the bedroom where I was held prisoner. I change direction, going out to the kitchen, back through the hallway, then into the lounge on a loop, stopping only when my leg is aching so much that I have to sit down. As I do so, I see Joe's car pulling up onto the drive.

When I open the front door to him, I'm normal; kissing him as I always do. The urge to show him the message the minute I see him is strong, because then he can reassure me, I can block the number and that will be that. But if I do that, he'll think that I don't trust him, that I'm doubting him.

I can't have that. I'll show him the message later, as if it's nothing, some sort of prank, drop it casually into the conversation as if I've just remembered it.

'So you had a good time with Zari?' He's shrugging off his jacket, easing off his shoes.

'It was great. I felt normal again, back to how life should be. We had such a laugh. Drank a fair bit of wine, too.'

'See? That's what you need, a bit of proper life. I think that's why it's been easier for me because I have work to go to and you know what that's like – a few hours back and it's as if you've never been away.'

'I'm looking forward to getting a job,' I tell him. 'Something permanent. Something worthwhile that I can progress in rather than temping.'

He pulls me to him, wrapping his arms around me.

'You seem better, more your old self.'

'That's the wine.' I laugh.

I relax into his arms but it's there, the thought; *Tell him about the stupid message. Put it to bed. Do it now.*

'I'm going to take a shower and get changed, then I'll make us a sandwich or something, yeah?'

'I'll make the sandwich while you take a shower, because you've been at work all day whereas I've done nothing except go out for lunch.'

'Not going to argue with that.'

I go out to the kitchen while Joe heads upstairs. Opening the fridge, I stand in front of it, trying to decide what to make. It shouldn't be a big deal, should it, making a sandwich? Everything I do now seems to be a massive decision, no matter how trivial the choice.

Maybe I need counselling.

Except that I can't ever tell anyone what happened, can I? Although don't counsellors have to keep everything confidential? I'm sure they do.

Yeah, but what if they don't?

Taking a packet of ham and the cheese from the fridge, I decide the best thing is to ask Joe what he wants and I'll have the same as him, because then I don't have to decide.

Pathetic.

When I get upstairs to our bedroom, the ensuite door is closed but there's no sound of the shower running. I'm about to tap on the door when I hear Joe's voice. I can't make out his words because he's speaking quietly. He must be on his phone.

Who is he speaking to?

Unsure what to do, I stand there, feeling as if I'm intruding somehow. That's ridiculous, isn't it? Don't be so stupid, Beth, there's no law that says he can't take a phone call while he's in the bathroom. I rap loudly on the door, as if I've just arrived and haven't been hanging around outside.

'Yeah?' he shouts.

'Ham or cheese?' I shout through the door.

He pulls the door open. 'Ham,' he says with a grin. 'You can come in, you know, it's not like you haven't seen it all before.' He has his shirt off, his trousers undone.

'Were you on your phone just now?'

He looks surprised. 'No, why?'

'I thought I heard you talking.'

'Haven't got my phone in here.' He gives me a strange look and I realise how weird I must sound.

'I'm obviously hearing things. Ham it is, then. I'll leave you to it.' I laugh and pull the door closed, but as I walk through the bedroom, I can't help from looking around to see where his phone is. I can't see it.

That's because it's in the lounge, Beth, and when you get downstairs and see it, you can feel truly shit for doubting him.

Except that when I get downstairs, I can't find his phone, because, shamefully, I go straight into the lounge to look for it.

It's not there.

To complete my disloyalty, I check his coat pockets, too.

It's not there either.

◆ ◆ ◆

Joe and I spent the evening catching up on a Netflix series, crashed on the sofa, snuggled up together.

A normal evening.

I didn't show him the anonymous message and now here I am, lying wide awake in bed, my mind going over and over every detail of the evening whilst he's snores beside me, fast asleep.

When he came downstairs after his shower, he'd changed into a t-shirt and joggers, and I knew he had his phone in his pocket because I could see the bulge. So the phone must have been in the bedroom for him to have put it into his pocket when he got dressed.

Except if it was in the bedroom, why didn't I find it? He would have slung it on the dressing table or bedside table. He wouldn't have put it away in a drawer, which means he must have had it in the bathroom.

So why did he lie about it? Or did he? Because I remember his expression now; he looked puzzled when I asked him if he'd been on the phone, not guilty.

Unless he's a very good actor.

Like Quinn was.

I stared at the television all evening, but I may as well have been looking at a blank screen because none of it went in, not one bit of it. All I could think about was that message and whether Joe was cheating on me and the more I thought about it, the sicker I felt. Not just at the thought of him cheating, but at myself for suspecting him. Yesterday, I had no doubts, today, because of a message from a random nutter, I'm doubting my husband.

What does that say about me?

Nothing good.

A week ago I thought we were both facing death and after the miracle of both being released, I'm allowing trivial nonsense to mar our freedom.

But even knowing that, it doesn't stop my mind from asking questions, looking for evidence of his betrayal. Does Joe normally keep his phone in his pocket or does he leave it lying around? Because he kept it in his pocket all night and I racked my brains to remember if he did that normally, but I couldn't remember. I've never taken any notice of what he does with his phone because it's never been important, but now, suddenly, it is.

I need to know but I can't exactly ask him, can I? So I've no way of finding out.

He never looked at his phone all night. I noticed that, never once took it out of his pocket to so much as glance at it. Or did he wait until he went out to the kitchen to get a drink to have a look? Maybe he did.

I think he did.

Because his phone never bleeped at all and mine did, which wouldn't mean anything except that I know he would have had the same message that I received, because we're in the same WhatsApp group with some friends, so he'd have received the message, too.

So he definitely had his phone on silent.

Does he usually do that? Again, I've never noticed but I'm thinking that he never used to, but he does now. Why would he do that?

Because he's been to work all day and he has it on silent there. I used to do that, didn't I? Just like we always put them on silent when we go to bed.

Perfectly valid; so I'm overreacting and being completely disloyal by suspecting him. One random, anonymous message and I'm ready to believe the worst of someone I love?

Ridiculous.

And yet once the seed of doubt takes root, it grows and telling myself that Joe is nothing like Quinn doesn't help. It sounded as if he was talking to someone when he was in the bathroom, or did I imagine that? Am I going mad and my brain is hearing things that aren't there?

So as I stared at the TV screen, my mind veered between being convinced that Joe's having an affair and then the next second, cursing my stupidity and paranoia for even *thinking* it. By the time we came upstairs to go to bed, I had a pounding headache and felt as if I was going to throw up. I stayed in the bathroom pretending that I was brushing my teeth for so long that by the time I came out, Joe was fast asleep.

Which is what I wanted, because if he'd tried to cuddle up with me, I'm not sure I wouldn't have blurted it out to him and I want to avoid that.

Why did I open that bloody message? I should have just deleted it like a normal person.

Unable to lie here anymore, I slip out of bed. Perhaps if I go downstairs and make myself a hot drink, when I come back I'll be able to sleep. I pick up my phone from the charger on the bedside table and take it with me.

Because I'm going to delete that message and

forget all about it. consign it to the bin where it belongs. Pretend that I never received it because it's rubbish, junk, spam.

Once in the kitchen, I flick the kettle onto boil and open up my phone screen.

To find another message.

He's a liar. You know it. You just don't want to believe it.

CHAPTER EIGHTEEN

'Why are you up so early? You don't have to go to work. You should make the most of it and have a lie in.' Joe slides two mugs of coffee onto the table.

'I need to get up and about and do some job hunting.'

'Well, there's no rush, but if that's how you feel, go for it. Toast?'

'Not for me, I'll get something later,' I lie. Right now, the thought of eating anything is unthinkable. Zero appetite is back in my life and the thought of yesterday's lasagne makes me want to throw up.

Watching Joe as he moves around the kitchen, I feel almost detached from reality, as if I'm studying a film, assessing an actor. Joe's good looking, there's no doubt about that. He has classic features, skin that is always blemish free and lightly tanned, and thick wavy hair. Tall and slim, he pretends he's a nerdy accountant but is far from it; his regular gym sessions keep him toned and fit and he's never been one to over indulge, except, occasionally, with alcohol. He's upped his gym sessions over the last few months because he says he has to work extra hard because his job is sedentary and he doesn't want to end up flabby and overweight.

Has he met someone at the gym?

Has a woman with a gym honed body made a play for him? Is he sick of me hobbling around and being negative and has been having fun with someone else? Or maybe he's met someone at work; there are lots of attractive women working at Torrington's. When we first met, I couldn't believe my luck that he was still single; that he hadn't already been snapped up because he's hot, there's no denying it. When we started going out together, it felt so good to be with him, as if I was the chosen one, because he was a popular guy and had already been out on dates with several of his work colleagues. He could have taken his pick of the eligible women there, but he chose me.

'What do you think?' Joe's looking at me from across the table.

'Sorry, I was miles away.' I manage a smile.

'Not brooding, I hope?'

It catches me, for a minute, his remark. Does he know, somehow, what I'm thinking, what I suspect him of? But then I realise that, of course, he's talking about 'that weekend,' not the text message.

'No, I'm not. Just thinking about my job quest, that's all. Going over in my head how I approach it. Normal stuff. Anyway, what do I think about what?'

'Fixing up to go out for dinner at the weekend with Tom and Zari? It's Tom's birthday next week and I know he'll want to celebrate but he'll be waiting for us to say about it. Friday or Saturday night? You know what a big kid he is if anyone forgets his birthday. Thought I'd suggest that new Chinese place, supposed to be really good food.'

'Great idea. We should book a table before it gets full up.'

'I'll message him. Make sure they're free.' Joe gets up, walks over to the dishwasher, opens it and puts his plate and cup inside.

The perfect husband. Would he do that if he were cheating?

He might do, nasty voice says, *to ease his guilt. Has he bought you flowers, too? Been extra considerate?*

'See you tonight.' He leans down and kisses me on the cheek. 'Don't overdo the job hunting.'

I laugh. 'No chance of that.'

When I hear the front door close, I get up and wander into the lounge to watch his car pull off the driveway before going out into the hallway and bolting the front door. Because that's what I do now; bolt the doors. But today, I'm not bolting them just because I'm paranoid about *them* breaking in, I have another reason, too.

I don't want Joe to be able to get into the house without me knowing if he should come back early from work.

It's unlikely; he never normally comes back once he's left for the day, but there's always a first time, and I don't want that time to be today.

Because I have stuff to do that he can't ever find out about.

I cross the hallway to the study, the room Joe and I use as an office. My laptop is in there and Joe's computer, too, set up on the worktop that runs the length of the room underneath the window. It has everything a home office needs with a printer, two luxury swivel chairs, two filing cabinets, and a radio that's rarely switched on. Neither of us uses it very much, me because I've been temping, which doesn't offer work from home as an option, and Joe because he's always preferred to go into the office. Joe believes if you work from home, you miss too much of what is going on. The stuff that's not actually work but is so important to progression; the office politics and intrigue that means you're out of the loop if you're tucked away at home.

Or maybe there are other attractions that I don't know about that tempt Joe to go in every day.

Shut. Up.

The study door is closed and I stare at my fingers resting on the doorhandle. Once I open this door, I'm committed. I'm admitting to myself that I believe Joe is capable of cheating on me.

Because I'm going to open his emails and search them.

What, exactly, am I looking for? I'm not sure, but something that will prove his innocence or guilt.

Am I really going to do this?

Yes, I am. Pushing down the handle, I open the door and go inside, closing it behind me. Go through his emails and get it over with, Beth, and then you'll know, one way or the other.

I settle down at his computer, turn it on, and log on. Joe's passwords to everything are jotted on a pad lying on the desk, where they always are. That's a good sign, isn't it, that he's not trying to hide his passwords? If he had something to hide, why would he make it so easy for me to check on him?

Because he thinks you won't bother, nasty voice says, *he's sure of himself.*

Navigating to his emails, I push down the guilt and scroll through them. Nearly an hour later, I've found nothing. I've gone back over the previous six months and found nothing incriminating; no emails to a female colleague that are overly friendly, nothing out of the ordinary, nothing to make me suspect that he's been doing anything or seeing anyone he shouldn't, no secret hotel bookings when he's been away for work conferences, nothing in the slightest bit suspicious.

But would there be? He's hardly going to email a woman to make arrangements, is he? No one uses email for socialising.

If only I could get into his phone.

But I can't; there's no way I can see what's on his phone except by doing it in the middle of the night when he's asleep.

Am I really going to stoop so low?

No.

Maybe.

Closing down his emails, I'm about to log out of the computer when I spot a bookmark for his credit card. Joe uses that card to pay for absolutely everything, preferring to pay for it all in one go when his statement comes in. He only uses his bank account to draw out cash and very rarely does that. Like me, he hardly ever uses cash and uses his credit card on his mobile for everything. If he's been spending money on another woman, that's where it'll be. Any meals out or gifts for a secret lover will be on there. Finding his password on the notepad, I tap on the bookmark and log in. Dreading what I might find, I go back months, scrolling through hundreds of entries and scrutinising every item to see if there's anything out of the ordinary.

I find not one thing that shouldn't be there; not one single thing.

Sitting back in the chair, relief washes over me, along with shame at doubting Joe. Why did I allow two stupid anonymous messages to make me doubt him? I feel sick and dirty for probing through his emails and credit card statement.

Why did I ever think, for even one second, that Joe would cheat on me?

Picking up my phone, I find the messages and, without reading them again, I delete them and block the number. If any more messages come through from a withheld number, I'll do what I should have done in the first place – delete them immediately. Whoever is sending them is sick and just trying to cause trouble.

Why delete them? Why not show them to Joe?

Because they're rubbish and they don't merit being talked about, but mostly, I don't want Joe to know that I've doubted him. How can I show him those messages and talk about them when I've been checking behind his back? I won't be able to look him in the eye, knowing what I've done.

I'm the cheat, not Joe.

Joe knows how Quinn behaved and how he treated me. Infidelity is something that we both have strong views on; if you cheat on your partner, it's all over anyway because you can't love them if you do that. I feel so guilty about what I've done now and the only excuse I'm giving myself is that after that weekend, I'm not thinking straight. Shouldn't I be feeling incredibly grateful that Joe and I have our lives back? That we're alive? Instead of fixating on nonsense?

I am grateful and I've not been thinking straight.

It stops now. No more.

Joe would never, ever cheat on me and I've seen the proof for myself. I get up, tuck the chair underneath the countertop, go out of the room and close the door.

It's done. Over.

◆ ◆ ◆

It's the dream that wakes me, but the details of it have already gone, drifting away into the night like smoke. No matter how I try to grasp hold of them, they're elusive, a vague memory of taunting me from the edge of my consciousness. Lying in the darkness, Joe's steady breathing the only sound, the warmth of his body next to mine, is familiar, comforting, safe. It's one of the many things I love about him, the fact that no matter the weather, he's always warm. Joe's body has its own micro climate and no matter how cold I am, he's always toasty. I smile to myself; yesterday was a good day as I was determined that it should be after my snooping. After applying for a couple of jobs, I got a cab and went shopping; buying expensive steak for dinner, along with a luxury dessert and a bottle of our favourite wine. Date night; something we haven't done since *before.* I was embarrassed by my snooping; by what I'd done and glad that Joe will never know how I let him down. When we came upstairs to bed, we made love, and it was just as good as it always was, better, even. Joe whispered that he loved me and when I replied that I loved him, I meant every word of it.

Altogether, it was the perfect evening.

So go back to sleep.

But I can't, because whilst I can't remember the dream, I've remembered something else, something that my subconscious has refused to bury and has now forced its way into my head. A nagging question that demands to be answered. I didn't want to remember it, but now it's stuck, refusing to go away.

When I searched Joe's emails, I found no emails that shouldn't be there, not one, nothing. His credit card statement, too, had no unexplained purchases, no meals at fancy restaurants, no expensive gifts from fancy shops that I never received.

Nothing.

Except that it's not about what I found, it's what I *didn't* find.

There was no email from the hotel for *that weekend*, the spa hotel that Joe booked as a surprise for our anniversary. There should have been one, shouldn't there? I remember Joe saying that they'd sent directions to him on how to get there after he'd emailed and requested them, after they'd confirmed our reservation. He made a big thing about me not knowing where we were going; that we didn't need the sat nav because he had an email with all the information he needed. He was doing it the old-fashioned way, he said, and keeping it a surprise.

So there should have been several emails from the hotel, shouldn't there?

There weren't.

Okay, he could have deleted them.

He could, but if he did, where are they? It was only a couple of weeks ago, they would still be in the deleted folder, and they weren't because I checked. And I didn't find any email that he sent to them either, because I checked all his sent emails, too.

So there was no email to or from the hotel.

Okay, so maybe he deleted the deleted emails, to completely erase the memory of *that weekend* and make it as if it had never happened. That's completely possible, because I might have done that, so Joe could have, too.

Except that there was no credit card payment for the hotel either, because I checked. Even if the hotel had refunded the cost, and I don't think they would because we were a no show, the entries would have been on the online statement.

And they wasn't.

Which means Joe lied.

Why? Why lie about booking a weekend away? I can't think of a single reason why he would do that.

Or maybe I can, and I just don't want to face it.

Because it would be so much worse than Joe cheating on me.

CHAPTER NINETEEN

Joe

I knew who Beth was when she started temping at Torrington's.

Not that Beth knows that.

CeCe in HR told me before Beth even started work, but I had to keep quiet because if it got out, that leak would have cost CeCe her job. We dated for a while, me and CeCe, a *friends with benefits* type of thing, and she told me a lot of stuff she shouldn't have. She doesn't work at Torrington's now because her loose tongue finally got her the sack. HR don't want details of salaries and bonuses getting out because it causes upset and when someone told them CeCe was spilling facts like there was no tomorrow, it didn't take a lot of investigating to discover that she'd broken her contract a million times over. She was gone before you could say non-disclosure agreement. They didn't even allow her to clear her desk; she was marched out of the building by a security guard.

The someone who anonymously reported CeCe was me, but I don't feel guilty about it because she should have kept her mouth shut, shouldn't she? Also, she had to go because I didn't want her blabbing to the entire workforce who Beth really was and ruining everything for me.

So while Beth thought she was starting a new under-the-radar life, the fact was, I was well aware of who she was, or rather, used to be, but unlike CeCe, I kept my mouth shut. Unluckily for Beth, CeCe is a big celeb column fan and even though Beth looks so different from when she was Lizzi – brunette now instead of blonde; more natural and prettier, not made up because she doesn't need all the false stuff, CeCe had an inkling that she recognised her. Beth had a new passport with her new name on because she'd changed it legally, but that didn't stop CeCe. She did some digging around and matched up her birthdate and place of birth, because you can't fake stuff like when you're looking for a job. The fact that Beth was going by her middle name and her late mother's maiden name confirmed everything for CeCe, because they were facts that she could easily check and they confirmed her suspicions.

Which means I knew how rich her father was right from the start.

But that's not why I got with Beth. No way. I'd have fallen in love with her even if she were poor because what's not to love? She's gorgeous, kind, funny and sweet, not spoilt in any way at all. Perfect, in other words.

But I'm not going to lie. Her father being rich didn't put me off.

It's a fact that only rich people think that money doesn't buy happiness and that's because they've never had to go without anything. I know different. Beth has never had to go without. She went to a private school, grew up having expensive holidays and never wanted for anything. She doesn't know what it's like to be skint, to wear cheap clothes or worn out hand-me-downs, to go to school in a pair of second-hand shoes. She has no idea how it feels to have people look down their noses at you because you live in a rough area and drop your aitches. I know, because I come from a poor background and have had to use my looks and ability to claw my way out of a shithole sink estate.

People with money have the attitude that everyone has the same opportunities if you work hard enough, but people like me know the truth; you don't. Private school education opens doors to possibilities that a comprehensive never will. The old boy's network is very much alive and thriving, even if nobody wants to admit it. I know how hard it is to break the cycle of life on benefits. Poverty is wearing. It grinds you down and there is no hope for a better future when all you're doing is scraping by on barely enough money to put food on the table. Ambition to a poor person is having a few quid in your pocket by the time the next benefit payment comes around.

I never wanted to live like that.

I've erased my past; dropped the accent of my childhood and adopted a way of speaking that makes people assume I'm middle class. I dress well and I have a career; I was the first person in my family to go to university. I gave myself a future.

I never went back home after my first term at university; when I wasn't studying, I was working a couple of part-time jobs, and I had no time for family anymore. Was I being cruel? Maybe; but I had to break free and start afresh. I'd worked so hard to get good grades to get to university, suffered bullying at the hands of my classmates for being a swot because in their eyes, I was a swot, a weirdo for wanting to better myself. I had few friends when I was growing up, but I didn't care because I'd be leaving them behind, too, when I started my new life.

When I graduated, I never invited my parents to watch me receive my degree. They'd given up trying to contact me by then, too distracted with my elder brother's wild behaviour and his imminent prison sentence for drink driving. They had more important things to do than chase me for contact whilst I stubbornly ignored them. Whilst I felt a little sad during the ceremony as I watched everyone else's proud parents watching on, I consoled myself with the fact that this was just a few hours of one day. What did it matter when I had the rest of my life to look forward to? There was no point in thinking how proud my parents were that I went to university, the first member of our family to do so, the only member of our family because that was the past; now I had a proper future.

My parents never came to mine and Beth's wedding because I told Beth they were dead. I told her my father died when I was a teenager and my mother a few years before we met from cancer. Is that shocking? That I denied their very existence? That the real reason I discarded them was because I'm ashamed of them; embarrassed by their cheap clothes, my father's chain smoking, my mother's home-dyed hair, the way they speak? That I was afraid they would leech off me, ask me for money, expect help?

No; it was better this way, for me and for them and my two brothers. We were never a close family, even as children us brothers fought for attention and whatever money there was in our house. Me, the middle of the three, being picked on by both for being different from them, for having stupid ideas about bettering myself. I moved many miles away from my home town and none of my family know the town I live in, let alone my address, because I don't want to be found by them.

Not that they'll ever look.

I didn't need them; I had all I needed. I had Beth.

She's everything to me and I knew within days of meeting her that we'd be together forever, because we're soulmates. She was vague about her background and I never pushed her for details because, of course, I already knew. She told me her previous partner had cheated on her and how difficult it was for her to trust someone again. I told her then that I would never do that to her, that she was the only woman for me and I expected the same commitment from her. And then I asked her to marry me.

She was shocked; it was too soon, she said, because we'd only been together for a few months but I could tell she didn't mean it. I asked her what did time matter? When you knew, you knew. She felt the same way as me; we loved each other so why wait, I asked? I owned my own flat, she could move in with me and later I could sell it and we could move to a bigger place, start a family.

When she hesitated; I apologised, said that it was too soon, that I should never have asked and I was so sorry to have put her on the spot.

I begged her not to finish with me.

She laughed then and said she had something to tell me and then I could ask her again.

If I still wanted to.

She told me then about her father and his money and her previous life as 'Lizzi'. I pretended to be surprised, even laughed and said I didn't believe her. She showed me pictures of how she used to look and was completely taken in when I shook my head in disbelief. She told me how she wanted a real life, without anyone knowing who she was because once people knew, they treated you differently. She said she didn't care about money.

I sat silently as she told me and when she'd finished, she apologised for lying to me. I felt like shit, then, because I was the liar, not her, but I swallowed down my shame, got down on one knee and proposed.

And she said yes.

It was my suggestion that we get married in a registry office, that we tell no one, but if she really wanted the big wedding, we could wait while I saved the money to pay for it. I didn't want to do this, I told her, because it would mean a delay in being together properly and the way I saw it, the wedding reception would be for other people, not us.

All I want is you, Beth, I said.

At first, she was stunned that I intended paying for the wedding, but as what I'd said sank in, her shock turned to delight, because what she'd just told me had changed nothing and I still wanted her, not her father's money.

So we got married a few weeks later in a registry office, just the two of us with a couple of strangers off the street for witnesses. She rang her father that night and told him she was married and he was shocked, but he accepted it, because he had to. I knew he'd do anything for her and put her before anything else, despite his own feelings. It was done and nothing he could say would undo it, so he accepted it.

Or at least he appeared to.

Beth never knew the real reason I didn't want the big flash wedding that her father would gladly have paid for; I knew her father would interfere and stop Beth from marrying me.

Because I'd been doing research on James Winters and I knew he wouldn't be as trusting as Beth. He's very rich, and rich people guard their wealth carefully; he'd want to know all about this man who professed to love his daughter and whilst I've done nothing wrong, I have lied to Beth about my family. He'd be able to find that lie out easily if he cared to look and I didn't want that; it suited me for Beth to believe they were dead because to me, they are. I was afraid he'd expose my lies and put her off from marrying me, sow the seed of doubt, and I had to avoid that. Yeah, he could still do that after we were married, but he'd be taking a risk, wouldn't he? Because Beth's loyal to the core. Once we'd tied the knot, he'd have to tread carefully and not alienate her. But if he did tell her, I had a story all ready to tell her; a tale of childhood abuse, neglect, a past so traumatic that anyone would want to forget and we'd already be married by then.

James Winters may not be a full-fledged celebrity, but he still frequently appears in the media, even without Beth or Lizzi, by his side. For a couple of years there was always a buzz around him when Lizzi was with him, because nothing gets media attention like a beautiful woman. The press is always eager for a story and James Winters has a compelling backstory that gets retold with every appearance, often accompanied by photos of his late, beautiful wife. He's the millionaire mogul who never remarried after his wife passed away too young. At sixty-five, he's a striking figure and still handsome with a natural charm and a trustworthy face. He offers premium security services to pop stars and clients even wealthier than himself and some of that glamour has rubbed off onto him. But despite being a millionaire, I discovered that he comes from a poor background very similar to my own; he's a true self-made man. He's a businessman first and foremost; he'd protect his daughter and money carefully, so it was best if he found out we were married after the fact when he could do nothing to change it.

Because I knew if we'd told him before, he'd have made me sign a pre-nup.

And I couldn't have that.

◆ ◆ ◆

James Winters hated me on sight, as I feared he would. Not that he showed it.

He was polite to me, icily polite, but his insistence on calling me Joseph when I asked him to call me Joe was his way of getting at me. At first,

I sucked it up; pretended that I hadn't noticed, and went all out on the charm offensive.

It didn't work.

I know he had me looked into, not because he told me but because he'd drop remarks into the conversation about where I'd come from, ask me about my parents and then stare at me without blinking when I repeated the lie about them being dead. All done very cleverly so that Beth never noticed, but the minute she'd left the room, he'd start to question me again; ask where I'd gone to school, which university, ask me if I didn't wish I had brothers instead of being an only child, clamming up the minute Beth returned. He was letting me know that he knew that I hadn't fooled him for a minute.

So I gave up with trying to win him over because it was never going to happen. He disappointed me though, because when he's quoted in the media he's always banging on about being a self-made man and coming from nothing and yet he treats me like a gold-digger. No solidarity that we're the same, nothing.

So I call him 'mate' when I can, just to irritate him, because I know he hates it. Petty, I know, but it makes me smile when I see his annoyance.

He did buy us a house for a wedding present, though. Nothing too flash, a four bedroomed detached that we'd never have been able to afford on our salaries. He offered to buy us something much bigger but Beth refused; said that four bedrooms were quite enough, and she insisted that we sell our flats and put the proceeds into the house. That pissed me off a bit, if I'm honest. I could have rented that flat out for a tidy sum each month but Beth has this big thing about being 'normal' and not living off her father. I think that was when I realised that she was serious about it because until then, I'd assumed that after a while of living normally, the novelty would wear off and we could enjoy the lifestyle her father's money could give us. I thought she'd change, once we were married, let him help, but she was adamant. We didn't need her father's money, she said, because we were quite happy without it.

Which was true, but I'd be so much happier with lots of money.

But Beth wouldn't, and won't, accept anything else from him.

It took all of my persuasive powers to make her agree to use his luxury villa in Spain for a holiday. She absolutely didn't want to go; saying that she'd spent every summer of her childhood in that house and was bored with it. It was only when I told her how lucky she was that she'd had holidays every year, because I'd never been anywhere when I was a kid, that she relented.

So our lives carried on as normal and I had to accept that she wouldn't take anything from her father. We stopped talking about it because I didn't want her to think that it was important to me, even though it was. And I tried not to think about it, because when I did, I felt quite angry because she's wanted for nothing her whole life and I was basically dragged up. I won't lie, it rankled, the refusal to accept his money when there was so much of it to go around.

So I channelled that anger at the gym; used it to get myself a six-pack, punching that punchbag as if it were James Winters' face. I never even told any of my mates who Beth really was because she didn't want anyone to know how rich her father was. That was the other thing; keeping it a big secret got on my nerves because money's nothing to be ashamed of, is it?

It's a good thing.

So although on the surface everything between me and Beth was good, underneath, it festered. And one day, I blurted it out to Cole, my mate at the gym. Cole was a few years older than me, he was confident but not arrogant, with an easy smile that made conversation effortless. We'd started with casual nods between sets, then small talk about workouts, and before long we were spotting each other on the bench press and exchanging workout tips and had become good friends.

One evening, as we cooled down after a tough session, I found myself talking about more than just fitness. I didn't mean to open up about Beth and her father but one remark led to another and before I knew it, I'd confided it all in Cole. He listened without comment and when I'd finished, he said what I was feeling was perfectly normal.

And because he's not in our circle of friends, I didn't feel disloyal telling him, although I hadn't planned to, because he didn't even know Beth. Funnily enough, he works as a counsellor, so it didn't even feel like I was betraying Beth's trust about not telling anyone, because they're like priests, aren't they, counsellors? They don't go blabbing your secrets to everyone and even if Cole wasn't a counsellor, I knew he wouldn't repeat it because he was a mate. I felt so much better that I could offload how I actually felt instead of pretending I was fine with Beth's attitude to money. Cole totally got what I was saying and told me that I shouldn't feel guilty for talking about my feelings.

After that, we often chatted about it, although I'd lost hope that Beth would ever change her mind about accepting money from her father, but I told myself that it didn't matter, because I loved her. We talked of other things, too, but somehow, we always came back to Beth. Just after we came back from Spain and Beth had broken her leg, I confided in Cole that I thought Beth blamed me for her accident, because she hadn't wanted to go to her father's villa in the first place. She never said it was my fault, but I knew she thought it was. I could just tell. I didn't understand the big deal; if your father has a luxury villa standing empty, why wouldn't you use it? I said as much to Cole and he was quiet afterwards and I thought I should shut up and stop going on about it because he was clearly fed up with all the moaning. So I apologised and said he must be sick of hearing about Beth's father and the money, but he said, no, not at all, but that I needed to be honest with myself; that lying to myself about Beth's refusal to accept money from her father wasn't helping me. I replied that it didn't matter whether I was honest with myself or not; Beth wasn't ever going to change her mind, and that's all there was to it. But his words made me think about how I really felt and I was angry, I finally admitted, because I couldn't understand Beth's reasoning.

Cole looked at me then, as if he was deciding something, so I asked him what was wrong and he said that if I really wanted us to have some of her father's money, he could help. I laughed and asked him how? Was he going to talk to Beth and persuade her to see my side of things? He didn't laugh but looked at me with a serious expression and told me that I had a decision to make; if I wanted his help, I had only to say the word, but once I'd said it, I was committed. Intrigued, I said that of course I wanted his help, certain that there was nothing he could do.

'Are you sure?' he asked. 'Because there's no turning back once this is started.'

'I'm sure,' I replied, confident that there was no way he could help me.

And that was it; it was done.

The thing that nearly killed me and Beth.

CHAPTER TWENTY

'Are you okay?' Joe says as he leans down to kiss me on the lips.

I don't answer, because I can't; right now, I'm having trouble even looking at him, let alone speaking to him.

'What's wrong?' He studies me with concern, a slight frown on his face. 'You don't look well.'

'Awful headache,' I choke out the words.

He sits down on the chair next to me and pulls me into his arms.

'Hey, I can stay home and look after you, you know. It's not a problem.' He rubs my back, and I fight the urge to push him away.

'No need,' I say, pulling away from him and standing up. 'I'm going back to bed to sleep it off.'

'You shouldn't have got up. Get back into bed and I'll bring you up a hot drink, yeah?'

'No, it's fine. I don't want anything to drink. I just need to sleep it off.'

He looks confused. Probably because I'm snapping at him as if it's his fault that I'm ill.

It is his fault, although I'm not ill; I'm angry. And frightened.

I've been down here in the kitchen since five o'clock this morning. Although I told Joe I'd got up just before him, I was unable to sleep and couldn't lie there any longer and came down here to work out what I'm going to do. I've been thinking for so long and getting nowhere that my brain feels as if it's about to explode. My thoughts have veered between telling myself to stop being so ridiculous as to even think that Joe had something to do with the kidnap, and the next minute I'm convinced that he must have been behind it, because what other explanation is there? I should ask him so he can tell me I've got it all wrong, but I'm not sure that I can trust him now. No matter what he says, would I believe him?

'Beth?'

'I'm okay, honestly, I just need to go back to bed.' This time I even manage a smile when I say it. You deserve an Oscar, my brain tells me, because right now I want to scream and shout at him; beat him with my fists until he tells me what the hell is going on.

'You sure?'

'Yep.' I flap a hand at him as if waving goodbye and walk quickly into the hallway and up the stairs, afraid that he'll guess that there's something much more wrong with me than a headache.

'You sure you don't want me to stay home?' he calls from the bottom of the stairs.

'No. Go to work,' I say, without turning around. 'There's no point in you staying home. I'll be in bed.'

'I'll call you later. Check you're okay?'

'Message me,' I call out as I trudge robot-like into our bedroom. 'In case I'm asleep.'

I flop onto the bed and close my eyes. When I hear the front door closing, I immediately get up and go to the bedroom window, pull the curtain aside, and watch as Joe reverses off the driveway. He drives down the street and pulls onto the main road and when he's disappeared from sight, I go into the bathroom. Stripping off my pyjamas, I step into the shower and stay there until the water runs cold, forcing myself to stay under the freezing spray until I can stand it no longer.

By the time I'm dressed, I've formulated a plan, of sorts. The first step is to check with the hotel to see if Joe booked the weekend for us. He could have deleted the emails and paid for it another way and never used his credit card. I'm pretty sure he said the hotel was called The Swanhope, so it'll be easy to find their number if I look on the internet. Just because I couldn't find an email or a credit card entry doesn't mean he's guilty.

Guilty of what, Beth?

Having me held for ransom. Because incredibly, that seems the only explanation if he didn't book that weekend away because it would mean he knew we would never arrive at the hotel. But I haven't let myself think beyond that, because I can't cope with truly believing that Joe has betrayed me.

There has to be an explanation for no record of him making a booking. I just need to find it.

Snapshots of that weekend keep coming back to me; Joe's battered body, his bruised face, his chipped tooth, the rough way they dragged him away and threw him in the back of the truck as I watched from the window. He'd clearly been beaten, and there was nothing fake about his injuries.

Yeah, but they had to make it look real, didn't they?

It didn't just look real; it *was* real, and so was Joe's anger at them when they took me to see him at the trading estate. He definitely wasn't faking that.

So maybe I'm going mad.

It's possible, because I feel as if I am.

They were a lot of people involved in what happened that weekend. Evan and Mick and who knows how many others at the trading estate. Do I honestly believe that Joe arranged a gang of men to hold me hostage to make Dad pay the ransom? How would he even go about doing something like that? Joe's an accountant, not a criminal mastermind. I'm pretty sure that, like me, he would have no idea where to even start.

I don't know what to believe. A sudden urge to pick up the phone and talk to Dad washes over me. He'd know what to do; he'd sort everything out and find out what was going on. He'd make everything alright again.

But what if I'm wrong? What if there's a perfectly innocent explanation for it all? What if I'm overreacting and panicking, just like I did when I was trapped in the car and started screaming?

It's possible.

How disloyal it would be to go behind Joe's back and ask Dad to investigate him. If Joe found out, he'd never forgive me and I couldn't blame him for that. Involving Dad now would show him I don't trust Joe and that I was wrong to marry him without speaking to him about it first. Dad's never really forgiven me for not telling him we intended to marry. For springing my marriage on him, as he put it. He was hurt, said that it implied I didn't trust him. He wasn't far from the truth; one of the reasons Joe and I kept our wedding a secret was because I knew that if I told Dad, he'd have hijacked our wedding under the guise of making sure that I was okay. A prenup would have been forced on me and he'd have checked into Joe's background and questioned him relentlessly. I'd have been in the middle of the two of them and I wanted to avoid that.

No, I have to be certain before I speak to Dad;

do everything I can to find out the truth about that weekend. Once I've rung the hotel to see if Joe booked us a room for the weekend, the decision will be made for me. If he booked us a room, then that's the end of my stupid suspicions and I can spend the rest of my life being disgusted with myself for doubting Joe.

My phone rings, shattering the silence of the room and the clattering in my head. I pick it up to see Joe's name on the screen. I don't answer it but stare at it until it stops ringing.

Not now, Joe, I can't speak to you now.

Because I have things to do.

◆ ◆ ◆

'I just need a copy of the booking, as I'm going to claim on our holiday insurance. We couldn't travel to you because of the snow, you see.'

'So it was for two nights for the weekend of the twenty-eighth of January?'

'Yes.' I lie. 'But as I explained to your colleague, I need a receipt to make the claim and I've mislaid the email.'

'Just one moment.' Classical music replaces her voice and I sigh impatiently. I've explained the same lie twice now; once to the man who answered the phone and now to Phoebe, his supervisor, who he passed me over to. He seemed concerned that I was after a refund, but I've been at great pains to impress on Phoebe that I'm not.

The music stops, and she's back on the line again.

'Can I check your name again, please?'

'Beth Coburn, but the booking could be under my husband's name of Joseph.'

'One moment, please.' The music clicks in again and I'm suddenly hopeful. If there was no booking, she'd have told me by now, wouldn't she? Maybe Joe used a different card, his bank card, maybe, because I never checked that. Have I set myself up for all this angst and suspicion when, if I'd simply checked his bank account, I could have saved myself from all of this?

'Mrs Coburn?' She's back again.

'Yes?'

'I've checked those dates, but I'm afraid I can't find anything under you or your husband's name. Is it possible that you've mixed us up with another hotel?'

'Oh, I was sure it was you, but perhaps I have. I'll double check with my husband.'

'Yes, that...'

She's still talking as I hang up.

Could I have got the hotel wrong?

No.

It was The Swanhope. Besides, there are no other hotels with a similar name in the Cotswolds because I've looked. Joe mentioned the name of it several times to Evan, and it stuck in my mind.

Did Joe make the booking under a different name? Is that possible?

Don't be stupid. Why the hell would he do that?

He wouldn't; I'm clutching at straws because I don't want to accept the truth.

Joe lied.

It's time to call Dad or confront Joe about it; ask him, see what he has to say for himself.

But before I do either of those things, I'll take one last look at his computer. It's a delaying tactic, I know that, but I'm going with it because when I confront Joe and tell Dad, I'll be destroying my marriage.

Isn't it already destroyed? Not only has Joe lied, he's done something infinitely worse.

He was involved in what happened that weekend.

My phone pings and I glance at it to see there's a message from Joe. He's messaged me several times already and I haven't noticed. I don't open it, but ignore it because I need to find out what's going on before I can respond.

I go into the study and sit down at Joe's desk and fire up his computer. What am I looking for?

Something that will prove to me he hasn't betrayed me, but whatever that proof could be, I have no idea. Maybe I got the name of the hotel wrong; it could have been a different hotel and Joe paid the bill with his debit card. Perhaps the name is nothing like The Swanhope and I've remembered it wrong. I navigate to his bank account bookmark and use the details from the notepad on his desk to log on. I scroll through the transactions, going back several months. By the time I log out of his account, I feel sick.

There's nothing on there.

I'm about to close the screen when I spot another bookmark for a different bank that I haven't noticed before; an online bank that neither Joe nor I have an account with. Why would he have a bookmark for that bank account? Has he opened a new account without me knowing? It's possible; he doesn't need my permission to open an account, although I'm surprised he hasn't told me. Hope suddenly surges through me; I've got the wrong hotel, and he paid for it with his new account. It's as simple as that. Picking up his notepad with his passwords on, I read through them but frustratingly, there's no entry for that account. I check again and when I flip over the page, it's there, written on the top of the next sheet. I click on the bookmark and quickly type the details into the login screen.

Account not found.

Disappointment surges through me. Maybe I miss-typed it. Slow down, Beth, try again and don't blow this by locking yourself out of his account. Concentrating and double-checking every keystroke, I carefully type in the username and password. This time, the screen shimmers for a second and then loads. The account is in Joe's name. There's no doubt about that. Fingers hovering over the keyboard, I feel faint and as if I'm somewhere else as I stare at the details on the screen. I'm still trying to make sense of what

I'm seeing when I hear the front door opening, followed by Joe's footsteps in the hallway. I realise I didn't close the study door and he'll see me in here.

'Beth', he calls when he sees me, oblivious to what I've discovered. 'I came home to see if you're okay, but clearly you're feeling better.'

I don't turn around at the sound of his voice but sit frozen, staring at the screen in front of me.

'Are you feeling better now? Why didn't you let me know? I was getting worried.' He's behind me. I feel his hand on my shoulder and as I turn to look up at him, I wish that right now, I could turn back the clock and go back in time. Make this never happen, make this all go away. If I'd never received that anonymous text message, would I ever have doubted him?

No, I wouldn't.

'What are you doing on my computer?' He sounds confused. 'Is your laptop broken?'

'No,' I say, my voice cracking, a painful lump in my throat.

He frowns, confused. 'What's wrong?' I can't speak but when Joe opens his mouth to ask me again, I finally find my voice.

'Look at the screen, Joe,' I say. 'And tell me why you have a secret bank account with one million pounds in it.'

CHAPTER TWENTY-ONE

'What are you talking about?' he asks, frowning.

I jump up from the chair, sudden rage flooding through me.

'That!' I shout, stabbing my finger at the screen. 'The million pound bank balance. The money you stole from my dad for having *your wife* held to ransom.'

'I don't have an account with a million pounds in it.' He looks bemused, as if we're having some sort of joke. 'Trust me, I wish I did.'

'That's the trouble, Joe. I don't trust you. I checked with the hotel, and you never booked a weekend away for us because you knew we'd never arrive.'

'Of course I booked it. They've made a mistake, that's all.'

'How did you pay for it?'

'On my credit card, the same way I pay for everything. Look, why are you checking up on me?'

'You didn't pay for it on your credit card or with your bank card either, because I checked those, too. You're a liar, Joe.'

'It's not what it looks like,' he says, the colour draining from his face.

'I think it's exactly what it looks like.'

Pushing past him, I go out into the hallway and up the stairs as fast as I can, ignoring the shooting pains in my leg as I go. Once in the bedroom, I pull a holdall from the top of the wardrobe, hurl it onto the bed and unzip it. Flinging open the wardrobe doors, I drag stuff from inside and throw it into the bag and pull it back out again because it won't fit in with the hangers still inside it all. Ripping the hangers from the clothes, I throw them with as much force as possible at the wall, where they land with an unsatisfying clatter. I want to break something, smash something into a thousand pieces, vent my rage.

Do something.

I can hear Joe downstairs in the hallway, the click of his footsteps as he paces up and down. What's he doing, thinking of more lies to tell me?

The pacing stops and there's the sound of him coming up the stairs, almost running. I continue my packing and try to calm my breathing.

'What are you doing?' He's standing in the doorway, his face ashen.

'What do you think?' I demand. 'I'm leaving you, Joe, because funnily enough, now I've found out what you've done. I no longer want to be married to you.'

'Beth, please...' He takes a step forward, but I raise my hand, stopping him.

"No more lies, Joe. You paid someone to kidnap me. I can't stay with someone I don't trust anymore."

'You've got this all wrong.'

'Have I? How do you explain a bank account with a million pounds in it? It's not as if you saved it up because your job isn't that well paid, is it?'

'I don't know what you're talking about. I don't have a secret bank account or a million pounds. I don't. I swear to God. You're mistaken.'

'Really,' I scream. 'Really? That's the best you can do? It's downstairs on your computer in black and white.'

'It's the truth,' he says quietly. 'I can't explain how or why it's there, but it's not mine.'

'Well guess what? I don't believe you. I've seen the evidence with my own eyes. Bank accounts don't lie, whereas you've lied about everything. Every bit of that so-called weekend anniversary present was a lie. There was no hotel break, no accidental break down. You planned it all, didn't you?'

'Please. Let me explain.'

'Explain? You can't explain this away. You *sold* me, Joe, for a million pounds. I hope it was worth it.'

Turning away from him, I go over to the chest of drawers, yank the drawer open and pull out a handful of underwear.

'I love you, Beth, more than anything. I've never lied about that.'

I go back to the bed, stuff the underwear into the holdall and zip it shut, swallowing down the tears that threaten to engulf me. Hefting the bag off the bed, I push past Joe and head down the stairs.

'Where are you going?'

I ignore him as he follows close behind me. When I get down into the hallway, I take my boots out of the cupboard and pull them on, holding onto the wall to stop myself from toppling over. My bad leg feels unsteady and weak as I balance on it, but I carry on. I can't put my walking boot on because I need to drive my car and right now seems like a good time to never put that damn boot on again.

'Please,' Joe begs. 'Don't go. Stay. We need to talk about this.'

'Talk about what? Talk about the fact that you wanted money and used me to get it? You had me held captive. I thought we were both going to *die*. People don't do that to people they love. I was fucking terrified, and *you* caused that. *You* did that.'

'Please…'

'I thought you were different, Joe, but it turns out you're just like Quinn, out for what you can get. Actually, you're worse, because he never had me kidnapped.'

'I'm nothing like Quinn, I promise you. Please, just stay for a while and I'll explain everything.'

'Okay, tell me where you got a million pounds from.'

'That's not my account. I didn't even know it existed. I have no idea where that money came from. Someone else must have done it.'

'That's pathetic. Don't embarrass yourself.'

'Honestly, I swear on my life that is not my account or my money and I have no idea why it's on my computer.'

'So who put it there?'

'I don't know, but it wasn't me.'

'So someone made an account in your name and paid a million pounds into it? Why would someone do that, Joe?'

'I don't know. I wish I knew, but it wasn't me, Beth, you have to believe me.'

He looks and sounds so sincere, I feel myself weaken slightly and he senses it.

'Come and sit down and we can talk about it,' Joe says.

I hesitate for a moment; I so want to believe that he had nothing to do with it, but I've seen the proof with my own eyes. A bank account with a million pounds in it in his name doesn't lie.

Because what possible explanation could there be for that?

'Beth?' He's looking at me with pleading eyes.

'Just give me a chance? Listen to what I have to say?'

'Only if you answer me one question.'

'Anything,' he says.

'Did you have anything to do with what happened that weekend? Did you know I was going to be held for ransom?'

He looks down, avoiding my eyes and doesn't speak, telling me everything I need to know by his silence.

With that, I turn and walk towards the front door and Joe makes no attempt to stop me. He stands there, watching, as I step out of the life we've built together, and pull the door closed behind me with a final click.

◆◆◆

As I pulled out of the driveway, Joe opened the front door and was standing in the doorway, his face full of regret. Part of me desperately wanted to stay, even though he'd betrayed me so badly. I should hate him, but it's not so easy to turn off love. When I could bear it no longer, I turned my head away from him, pressed my foot to the accelerator and, with my heart hammering in my chest, reversed off the driveway and drove down the street. My last view of Joe was in the rearview mirror, standing immobile as he watched me leave.

As I drive, it feels strange to be in control of a

car again, but as I eat up the miles, I'm becoming more confident, slipping into the old familiarity of driving without thinking too much about it.

But I have to force myself to concentrate on the road because it would be so easy to zone out and have an accident or worse, *cause* an accident. I'm grateful that my car is automatic, because there's no way I would be able to drive the hundred miles to Dad's house in London. My left leg is still too weak to keep pressing the pedal to change gear.

Joe's been ringing me constantly since I left, his name flashing up on the media screen on the dashboard but I don't answer, because what else is there left to say?

Nothing.

Joe sold me out; used me to get money. Doesn't it always come down to money in the end? Just like Quinn, Joe saw me as his chance to get what he wanted, not caring how he hurt me in the process or how traumatised I was from the whole ordeal.

Which leads to more questions. Did he know who I was and who my father was from the moment I met him?

That, more than anything, hurts the most, because if he did know, it means he never loved me, that everything we had was based on a lie. Did he marry me because he thought I was rich and we could have a different life? Was the life we had never enough for him?

I think back over the last year, the occasions when Joe was exasperated with me for refusing

Dad's offers of money and now I wonder if he was angry at me for a version of our life that never came to be. Maybe he had pictured that when we were married things would be different; that I'd accept Dad's money, and we'd have long holidays, expensive cars, a bigger house. Maybe he expected so much more than what we had. Is that what drove him to set up the ransom? Was he that desperate for money? I thought we were so happy and that we had a good life.

But I was wrong.

Yet again, I've been fooled. Just like Quinn, Joe was out for what he could get.

It starts to rain heavily, and the road stretches ahead in a blur of headlights and rain, the wipers dragging slow, tired arcs across the windscreen. My hands are gripping the wheel, knuckles white, but my mind is somewhere else – somewhere in the past, tangled in the wreckage of what used to be. The worst part is that I believed totally in Joe; believed every single word that he has ever said to me. I put my trust in him and whilst he smiled and said all the things that I wanted to hear, every word was a lie.

The streets pass in a blur as I enter the outskirts of London, but all I can see is Joe's face as I pulled off the driveway. The way he had looked at me; the look of devastation on his face. That was a lie, too, or maybe it was real because he's been found out, hasn't he? That will be the reason for his expression, not the loss of me, but the loss of the money he betrayed me for, because once I tell Dad what he's done, he won't rest until Joe is arrested and charged. He'll make it his absolute mission in life to get revenge on Joe for what he's done to me.

Do I really want that – for Joe to be destroyed?

I don't know, not yet, because I can't think straight. I blame myself because I should have known; should have seen the signs because it had happened before. But like before, love made me blind, and Joe was such a good actor, even better than Quinn, because I never doubted him for a moment. Not once. Joe's betrayal is so much worse. And now all I have left is an empty life, and a car filled with silence, and the weight of knowing that I was nothing more to Joe than a ticket to the good life.

What was his plan? Did he intend to leave me to enjoy spending the money or was he going to stay and think of more ways to extort more money from Dad? Was that million pounds just the beginning? Who knows what else he had planned. Are there no limits to what he's capable of doing? If Dad hadn't paid the ransom, would I have been killed? Does he have life insurance on me that I have no knowledge of? Would the final big payoff for him result in arranging my death, leaving him a rich man? Is he really capable of that, of having me murdered? A car accident or a hit and run would be easy after a kidnapping, wouldn't it?

I blink hard to stop the tears and concentrate on the road. It's not much further now. Soon I'll be at

Dad's and there'll be a hundred miles between me and the man who I thought loved me and the sham of a marriage that I so believed in. How Joe must have laughed at how easily he fooled me.

Concentrate, Beth, keep driving, keep your eyes on the road.

The streets are familiar now and on autopilot, I steer the car to Dad's street; to the house I grew up in.

The house I left just two years ago, so full of hope.

As I pull into the driveway behind Dad's Mercedes, the gravel crunching beneath my tyres, I'm relieved to see his car there because it means he's at home. There would be nothing worse than him not being here. I turn off the ignition and sit immobile, my hands gripping the wheel. I'm exhausted, spent, not just from the journey, but from the betrayal. The heartbreak. The sheer weight of it all. I thought I'd feel some relief when I got here, but now, staring at the house, all I feel is hollow, empty. And then Dad is there, opening the front door, standing there watching me, waiting with that paternal instinct that tells him something bad has happened without me needing to say a word.

I swallow hard, push open the car door and step outside on shaking legs and walk towards Dad. His eyes are filled with quiet concern and suddenly, the weight in my chest cracks, just a little. I open my mouth to speak but have no words and instead,

I step forward and fall into his arms, and as he holds me tightly, I let it all go.

I let myself break.

CHAPTER TWENTY-TWO

Joe

What a fucking idiot I am.

Beth didn't believe me when I told her that the bank account with a million pounds in it wasn't mine, and why would she? She discovered I never booked that weekend away, and she's convinced I betrayed her.

She's right, I did, but I never received a penny of that ransom, not one penny.

Looking back, if I'd made the booking at The Swanhope, maybe Beth would never have looked any further. I made a schoolboy error by not booking the hotel and now I'm paying the price; my stupid accountant head that told me not to waste the money on a room we would never use has cost me everything.

That, and Cole Foster.

It all goes back to him; the man I thought was a mate, a good friend. I confided in him about Beth's father and his money and I should never have done that. It was disloyal and I'm disgusted with myself now for betraying Beth like that. But Cole was so convincing, so persuasive when he told me his plan for making Beth's father pay us a million pounds. His plan was reasonable, non-threatening, clever.

No one would get hurt and Beth would know nothing about it until afterwards, when it would be shown to be a scam; an opportunist taking advantage of James Winters's wealth and his love for his daughter. No harm would be done apart from relieving a man who could easily afford it of two million pounds.

Looking back, I find it incredible now that I went along with it; that I foolishly believed there was any chance of getting away with it. Aside from that, what the hell was I going to do with a bagful of cash? I couldn't just walk into a bank with a million pounds and pay it into my account.

I wasn't thinking straight.

Cole told me not to worry about what to do with the cash. *There are easy ways around that*, he said; *it was a minor thing*, uttering the words with such confidence that I believed him. The plan was simple; book a romantic weekend away in a hotel, pretend to break down in the middle of nowhere and spend the weekend at a house where there was no mobile signal, no way for Beth to contact her father or, more importantly, for him to contact her. It was perfect; Beth would enjoy a weekend in the country and I'd be a million pounds richer. Cole would get a commission and the guys who organised it would get theirs. All very civilised. No one was going to get hurt.

Except for James Winters's pride.

He was the only person who was going to lose anything. He'd have a weekend of anxiety and lose two million pounds, but he could easily afford it. Two million is spare change to him and when the police questioned me and Beth, we would simply say our car broke down and a kind stranger offered us shelter. As far as we were concerned, nothing had happened to us except for a pleasant weekend in the country. James Winters would have fallen victim to an elaborate scam, and I won't lie – the thought of him being outplayed by a con artist was satisfying. I would thoroughly enjoy seeing him made to look a fool.

That's if he even involved the police, which I doubted. He's a proud man, so would he really risk telling the police and it being leaked to the newspapers? Would one of the biggest names in personal security to the rich and famous want his name plastered all over the front pages for being scammed?

I didn't think so, and neither did Cole.

The two of us spent weeks talking about it, planning where and how, Cole liaising with the shady people who would do the deed. It was exciting meeting at the gym to discuss it and there was a part of me that never truly believed it was going to happen. It felt as if we were playing a game because it seemed too easy, too ridiculous, to be true. As the date we'd agreed got closer, I became nervous, because Cole was talking as if this was really happening. I began having second thoughts. What if Beth found out what I'd done? What if her father wouldn't pay? What if I messed it up?

So many ifs.

Cole was stunned when I told him I'd changed my mind. He said arrangements had already been made – a house had been rented for the weekend, money had been spent, people had been sourced. His exact words: *staff engaged.* Of course, I could back out if I really wanted to, he assured me, it wasn't an issue. But there were costs to be covered; expectations of easy money had been set, so there would be a cancellation fee. If I transferred a hundred thousand pounds to him that day, we could call the whole thing off immediately.

A hundred thousand pounds.

As if. I didn't have that sort of money, or any way of getting it, so I had no choice but to go ahead with it.

That day, our first wedding anniversary, the unexpected snowfall felt like a bad omen. Travel warnings were dominating the news and Beth was nervous about the weather and driving in the snow. After leaving the pub where we had lunch, the snow was coming down heavily, but I carried on, insisting it wouldn't amount to much. I felt sick as I drove, because it felt like everything was going wrong and the weekend hadn't even started, but I had no choice. I had to go ahead with it.

The plan was simple and the car hadn't really broken down; I simply lifted my foot off the clutch slightly so that it wouldn't start when I pressed the button. Beth had no reason to think I was lying, because why would I? When I went off to the meeting point to meet Mick as arranged, I thought I'd be leaving Beth on her own for ten minutes at the most.

But I got lost.

The snow disorientated me; everywhere looked the same, and stupidly, I'd stopped too soon, too far away from the house. When Mick found me trudging along, getting increasingly desperate, it was a massive relief because I wasn't sure I'd even be able to find my way back to the car. I'll admit those dogs scared the shit out of me when I saw them; Cole never mentioned them when we were making the plans. I convinced myself they had to make it look real but those great beasts put me on edge.

We walked back to the car, which was miles away and by the time we saw it in the distance, I was frozen and exhausted. Mick went on ahead, striding through the snow as if it were nothing, which was a big mistake; because Beth was hysterical when she saw him. I didn't realise how long I'd been gone and the dogs clearly scared the shit out of her, too.

By the time Mick had got us to the house, I was having serious misgivings about it all. Mick didn't seem much like a kindly stranger who was offering us help; he barely spoke a word, and he looked as threatening as hell, especially with the two hounds from hell hanging on his every word.

But I'd was relieved to find that I'd got that wrong, because Mick was the 'help' and Evan was the main act. As we pulled up to the house, it was impressive, I'll give them that, and Evan played his part perfectly.

Even I believed his gentlemanly act and I knew he was a crook.

But Beth wasn't happy; almost from the moment we arrived, she was eager to leave. She kept complaining about the phone signal and Wi-Fi, and she was irritated that our phones wouldn't work. Cole had made sure they'd be out of action after I gave him our details, arranging for the service to be cut off for the weekend. I don't know how he did it, and I didn't want to know. As long as it couldn't be traced back to me, that was fine. I didn't know any of the 'finer details,' as Cole called them, because if James Winters chose to involve the police, I couldn't inadvertently slip up if I knew nothing myself. The only information I had was where I had to stop the car, the rest was as much a mystery to me as it was to Beth.

I assumed Beth would settle down and enjoy the house and the countryside but she was on edge the whole time. Evan didn't fool her for a minute and she sensed something was off about him almost immediately. When she caught him on the phone, she just wouldn't let it go no matter what I said. My plan for a relaxing weekend, treating the house like a free hotel, was falling apart. Beth made no secret of the fact that she wanted to leave as soon as possible, and Evan could see she felt that way, too.

Some of it was my fault; I was nervous and I drank too much and my tongue ran away with me. I boasted to Evan about Beth's dad – ridiculous really as he already knew – but I was enjoying myself. Foolishly, I relaxed too much. Evan was interesting and charming and I suppose I forgot it was all an act. When he made a big thing of recognising Beth, it surprised me, and I wasn't sure why he'd done that. I realised after that he was playing with us, having a bit of fun. But even if he hadn't done that, Beth was wary of him from the start and there was no persuading her otherwise.

That second night, when Beth said she wasn't feeling well and went to bed early, I'll admit I was relieved, because it meant by the time I went up she'd be fast asleep so we wouldn't have to talk about Evan. There was only one more day to get through and then it would all be over and we'd be back home.

And I'd be a million pounds richer.

At least that's what I thought. When I said goodnight to Beth, and resumed enjoying Evan's hospitality, I was oblivious to what was coming next.

◆ ◆ ◆

Evan drugged Beth to make her ill. He didn't bother drugging me, but as soon as Beth had gone upstairs, Evan got up from his seat and left the room. Bemused, I sipped my wine and waited for him to come back.

He didn't.

Mick came into the room with the dogs, yanked me out of the chair, and started shoving me toward the hallway. Stunned, I pushed him away and demanded to know what the hell was going on. His answer was to punch me in the face. The force of the blow sent me sprawling to the floor.

When Evan appeared in the doorway, I thought he'd come to help me, but I was totally wrong. He walked over to me as I lay on the floor and coldly informed me that if I had any sense, I'd do as I was told and not argue. I snapped back that he had it all wrong, that he was the one who should be listening to me, that Cole had arranged everything, and we were to be treated as guests and he'd better remember that.

He laughed then and said I wasn't the one giving orders and if I didn't comply, I'd end up as dog meat. Or worse, Beth would. The dogs were watching, ready to pounce, and the thought of what those enormous teeth could do to human flesh made me feel sick.

Mick dragged me down to the cellar with Evan following. He told me how it was going to be; I was no longer getting any of the ransom money and if I didn't like that, then too bad. As long as Beth's dad paid up, Beth and I would be freed, but if either of us even thought about going to the police, we'd both end up dead and they'd make sure it wasn't a pleasant death.

I was terrified. Not just for myself, but for Beth.

It was up to me, they said, to persuade Beth and her father not to involve the police, and they didn't give one shit how I did it. Mick punched me a few more times then, just because he could, but I didn't fight back, not then, because those dogs were there and I knew he just wanted an excuse to set them on me. When the door shut on me and I was alone in the darkness, I realised how incredibly stupid I'd been.

Because there's no honour among thieves.

In the following hours, I tried to think it through. Had Cole set me up, or had Evan and Mick got greedy and wanted more than their fair share? Not that it mattered, all I had to do was hold myself together and pray that Beth and I would get out of there alive. When Mick came back, I thought they were letting us go, that Beth's dad had paid the ransom, but they just moved me somewhere else. Some sort of warehouse after a journey from hell in the back of that truck, those fucking great dogs breathing on me and snarling every time I so much as twitched.

I thought I'd never get out of there alive; there were others involved, at least two, and once at the warehouse, Mick took great delight in giving me another kicking. I landed a few kicks on him myself this time, because I thought he was going to kill me, anyway. Although I paid for it with a chipped tooth and a black eye, seeing him wince was immensely satisfying.

I'll never forgive myself for what I did to Beth.

When they brought her to the warehouse, she was in such a state and I truly realised what I'd done. By then, I didn't care if they killed me. I just wanted Beth to be safe because she didn't deserve any of it, and it was all my fault. She was so terrified that she tried to escape by pretending to slash her wrists and that's on me, her terror, her fear. I'm responsible for that.

I made that happen.

When they took her away, I prayed to a God that I've never believed in to save her and take me; I made a deal that it didn't matter what they did to me as long as Beth was okay.

The next day when Mick arrived and put a sack over my head and put me in the car, I thought they were taking me to kill me. Maybe even dig my own grave. When I stumbled out of that car and Mick ripped the sack from my head, I couldn't believe my eyes.

I was home.

With every step I took up the driveway to the house, I was expecting a bullet in the back. I thought they were taunting me; teasing me, having a bit of fun before they finished me off. When Beth opened the front door and I saw her standing there, I honestly thought I was dreaming, imagining things.

But it was real; incredibly, they'd let us go.

Beth was desperate to call the police and I couldn't let that happen because that would be the end of us; those kidnappers would show no mercy. They'd come back and kill us. It was hard persuading her and when her dad turned up, I wondered how I was going to swing it because I thought he'd want to report what had happened too when Beth told him what had happened. A scam he'd let go, but keeping us prisoner? No. I couldn't see him not reporting that, so when he said no, he didn't think we should involve them, I was shocked. But then it hit me; how much he didn't want to lose face. The man who was supposed to protect everyone, admitting that he couldn't even protect his own daughter, would have been a humiliation he couldn't afford. He said we shouldn't call the police because the kidnappers were at the bottom of the food chain, and the people at the top would make sure they were never brought to justice. We'd be in more danger from the ones at the top, he said. Whatever his reasons were, I was relieved that he agreed; no police.

Life slowly returned to a semblance of normality. Not quite the same as it was, but close. Bruises fade, memories blur, time heals. Eventually, we would move on, and with time, it would fade away, as if it had never happened. We would put that weekend behind us, and in time, it would be forgotten. I had the rest of my life to make it up to Beth. She'd never know the truth about that weekend, and I'd do my utmost to make her happy. Too late, I realised I didn't actually care about money anymore; we have enough, more than enough.

We had each other.

Only now, we don't.

It's my fault, I know that, but not mine alone. Before I saw that account with a million pounds in it, I blamed Cole, assumed that he was the one who set me up because he's disappeared off the face of the earth. Once I'd recovered from that weekend, I tried to track him down but his phone number is no longer in use, he never returned to the gym and the flat he supposedly lived in – the address doesn't even exist. The counselling service he claimed to work for had never heard of him, either. Every moment that I could, alone in the car or in the bathroom, I made endless, useless phone calls to counselling services, gyms, anywhere I could think of, to trace him. Once, Beth nearly caught me and I decided then to let it go, because it was useless.

Cole Foster had vanished off the face of the

earth.

But although I blamed him, I've realised now that this isn't on him. He was just a lackey, the same as Mick and Evan and all the rest of them. The million pounds in the account I never set up – that changes everything. That's what told me who is behind this, who set me up.

Someone is out to ruin me, and there's only one person capable of setting up something like this.

And now I'm out for revenge.

CHAPTER TWENTY-THREE

I take a sip of the tea that Dad insisted on making me and grimace; it's loaded with sugar, a lot of sugar.

'It's for the shock,' Dad says, noticing my reaction.

'I haven't been in an accident, Dad.'

'You've had a shock, though, a nasty one. The sugar will help, give you some energy.'

I force myself to swallow it. The tension is beginning to ease from my shoulders, but I have a thumping headache and my eyes are swollen and sore from crying so much. I don't think I have any tears left. I've told Dad the whole sorry saga, and he listened, without interrupting once, and I'm grateful for that because I just needed to get it out, say the words.

Be done with it.

It must have been hard for Dad to listen to and, although he never spoke or commented, his clenched fists and rigid jawline told their own story. When I'd finished, he pulled me into a hug and I sobbed in his arms until I couldn't cry anymore.

So it's over. We're done. Joe can't possibly hurt me any more than he already has, and I'm back where I started.

Back home with Dad.

This room is warm, familiar and comforting, just as it always was. Nothing has changed, except for me. The pictures on the mantelpiece and table are just as they always were; me, my mother, my parents' wedding day, pictures of me as a baby and the whole of my life afterwards. This is home. Why was I ever in such a hurry to leave?

There's no picture from my wedding to Joe amongst the gallery, although I gave Dad one the registrar took for us. Maybe he always guessed the truth about Joe. Did he never take to him because he didn't trust him?

'You've not even surprised, are you?' I ask, putting my thoughts into words. Was Dad expecting Joe to do something like this from the minute I met him? Did he see him for what he was, whereas I was blinded by love? I should have trusted Dad and let him meet Joe before I rushed into marriage. Did I not allow that because I was afraid he'd burst my bubble of complete trust in Joe?

After a moment, Dad shrugs, but doesn't answer my question.

'You never liked him, did you?' I ask.

'I never said that. I didn't really know him, and you never gave me the chance to get to know him before you ran off and married him.'

'Well, that'll teach me, won't it?'

He sighs and pats my hand. 'Look, love, I take no pleasure in this. I'll admit I had my doubts about him from the start, but I kept them to myself because all I've ever wanted is for you to be happy. To have a happy life, a happy marriage like me and your mum had, short though it was. You have to realise that Joe's not the same as you and me. He comes from a rough background that he had to fight his way out of. I know that much because he told me. He never tried to hide it. People like that… they think differently from us.'

'You come from a rough background yourself. You've always said that's what's made you so determined to do well.'

'It did. Poverty spurred me on, but it can go either way. Some people work their socks off to succeed, like I did, and others, like Joe, chase the easy money, the get-rich-quick schemes. It's the way of the world.'

'Thanks. So I'm easy money now, am I?'

'That's not what I meant. You're twisting my words.'

'I know.' I sigh. 'Sorry for taking it out on you. It's not your fault I married a bastard.'

'You were unlucky.'

'Bit of an understatement,' I mutter. 'Not many husbands arrange to have their wives kidnapped so they can get themselves a million pounds.'

'We'll sort it all out, don't you worry. You can leave it to me and the lawyers. You won't have to do a thing. You never need go back to that house if you don't want to.'

Should I return or just walk away, leaving everything I own behind and start afresh? It's tempting, because it's the easier choice, but I know I need to confront things. Grow up. Being back here doesn't mean I should fall into old habits and let Dad take control of my life again and spend the rest of my life taking the easy option.

'I'll go back,' I say. 'But not while Joe is there, I'll wait until he's gone. First thing tomorrow morning, I'm going to the police to report what he's done because he shouldn't be allowed to get away with it.'

'That's tomorrow's problem. There's no need to think about it now. For now, finish your tea and I'll cook us something to eat in a while.'

'I'm not hungry.'

'You've got to eat. Starving yourself will do no good. I could make that nice pasta thing you like, you know, the mushroom linguine. It's my signature dish.' He smiles.

Maybe if I eat, it'll get rid of this awful headache because Dad's right, making myself ill will get me nowhere.

I have a life to rebuild.

'Doesn't Sally still come every day?' I ask.

'Just two days a week now. She's getting on and it didn't seem fair to make her come here every day when there's not a lot for her to do. She was delighted when I suggested it because she wanted a bit more time to spend with the grandchildren.'

'Getting on? She's only a couple of years older than you.'

'I know, but she seems older. Anyway, I can cook, you know. I don't starve and I go out to eat a lot, so there's no need for her to come every day. It's not like the place needs cleaning much with just me here.'

The doorbell shrills, and I look at Dad in alarm.

'Who's that?'

'I don't know,' he says, getting up from the sofa. 'Only one way to find out.'

He goes to the window, pulls the curtain back and peers outside.

'It's Joe,' he mutters, turning to me with a grim expression.

'Ignore him,' I say firmly. 'I've got nothing to say to him.'

'Well I have,' Dad says, heading towards the hallway. 'And it won't be pleasant.'

◆ ◆ ◆

The moment Dad opens the front door, Joe wedges his foot inside and tries to barge in, but Dad stops him with ease – even at sixty-five, his size makes him a force to be reckoned with.

'Let me in,' Joe shouts, his voice laced with anger. 'I want to see Beth.' I'm taken aback; I expected desperation, pleading – not fury.

'She doesn't want to see you, but I have a few questions,' Dad replies calmly.

Joe's response is to use his body to shove the door against Dad, but he doesn't budge.

'It's okay, Dad,' I say quietly from the lounge doorway. 'Let him in.'

'You can come in, as long as you watch your mouth,' Dad says, his tone steady and composed. Joe grits his teeth, glaring at him with pure hatred.

Dad looks at me and I nod. Opening the door, he steps aside to let Joe through, pulling himself up to his full six-feet-five as Joe walks past him.

I go back into the lounge and stand in front of the window, unwilling to sit down. Standing makes me feel steadier, more in control. Joe and Dad follow behind me, and Dad comes to stand beside me, crossing his arms.

'What do you want, Joe?' I ask, my voice cold. 'I don't think there's anything left to say, is there?'

'I'm sorry,' Joe says, his voice heavy with regret. 'Sorrier than I can ever say, but you need to know that I never took a single penny of that ransom money.'

He's admitting it. He staged the kidnapping. The words hit me like a punch to the chest. Until now, a tiny part of me had clung to the hope that there was some other explanation. But Joe's words have just shattered that hope completely.

'I love you, Beth. So much,' he continues. 'I made a terrible mistake, a stupid mistake, one I'll regret for the rest of my life. It was never meant to happen like this. We were just supposed to have a weekend away in the country and you wouldn't have even known about the ransom until we got back. It would have looked like your father had been scammed, nothing more. You would never have thought it was a kidnapping, just a scam.'

'A scam?' Dad roars. 'You think that's okay? That makes it better? So what happened, Joe? How did it all go so wrong, this harmless kidnapping of yours?'

'You bastard,' Joe shouts, stepping towards Dad, thrusting his face close to him. 'Don't pretend you don't know.'

'Watch your mouth,' Dad growls, his fingers curling into fists.

'You knew all about it,' Joe says, stepping back. 'So stop pretending.'

'Knew all about what? What am I supposed to know?' Dad asks. 'I don't know what you're talking about.'

'You fucking set me up,' Joe snarls at Dad. 'I would never have even thought about doing anything if you hadn't set me up.'

'You're not right in the head.' Dad looks bemused. 'I think you'd better leave.'

'Yeah, you'd like that, wouldn't you? You don't

want me asking awkward questions, do you?'

'Get out.' Dad steps forward and grabs hold of his arm. Joe rips his arm away and Dad's face flushes with colour; a sure sign that he's about to lose his temper.

'You need to leave, Joe.' I force myself between them.

'Beth, listen to me. Let me explain.'

'There's nothing more to say.'

'There is,' Joe pleads. 'Just hear me out and then I'll go. Please?'

I look up at Dad, then gently put my hand on his chest and push him towards the window.

'Okay,' I say to Joe. 'You've got five minutes, but you say your piece there. Don't move.'

Joe nods.

'Okay.' I stand next to Dad. 'Say what you have to say and go.'

Joe takes a deep breath.

'It started last year. I met this guy at the gym and we became friends. It was his idea, staging the kidnapping. He persuaded me to do it.'

I start to speak, to ask why he's blaming someone else, but Joe holds his hand up.

'Please, let me just tell you it all. I'm not making excuses or trying to shift the blame, but you need to know how it happened. I was weak, and it sounded easy; a million pounds for doing nothing more than enjoying a weekend in the country. No one would get hurt. It was the perfect plan.'

'Only we did get hurt, didn't we?' I say. 'And

terrified beyond belief.'

'I know.' Joe shakes his head. 'That wasn't meant to happen. I couldn't understand why it had gone so wrong. As soon as they'd locked you up, they told me there'd be no money, but if I was lucky, they'd let us live.'

'So you're trying to say you got scammed, too,' I say. 'Except you didn't, did you? Because you have a million pounds in your account.'

'No.' He shakes his head. 'I don't. It's a fake, Beth. That account you logged onto is fake. It doesn't exist. It's simply a page set up to look like a bank account. There is no money, no million pounds.'

'Right,' Dad says, stepping towards Joe. 'I've heard enough. Time for you to leave before I call the police and have them take you away.'

'You sound worried, *mate*,' Joe snarls at Dad. 'Frightened of what I'm going to say next, are you?'

'I'm not frightened of you, you little shit,' Dad says. 'And if you want to step outside, I'll show you how unscared I am.'

'Stop it!' I shout.

They both turn to me.

'You've got a bloody cheek,' I spit the words at Joe. 'You're the criminal, not Dad. So stop trying to blame him and just go.'

'He's done nothing wrong?' Joe snaps, surprising me with his response. 'You think? Well, there's stuff about him that you don't know. Ask him what his men were doing on my computer when they were fitting the new alarm. Ask him about Cole Foster.'

'What? I don't know what you're talking about,' Dad says.

'Who's Cole Foster?' I ask, as if it matters.

'The guy at the gym. The one who arranged everything, the one, *you...*' He stabs a finger at Dad. '...set me up to meet. Your Dad did it, Beth, he was behind it all, and yeah, I fell for it, which means I'm weak and don't deserve you, but he's the one who did it. He's the one who gave us a weekend of terror and frightened you to death. I'd never have done that to you. Never. He did it to break us up, and he didn't care how much he scared you in the process.'

The room is silent after his outburst and stunned, I look at Joe and then Dad.

'That's it?' I ask. 'You're blaming him for what *you've* done?'

'I'm not lying. It all makes perfect sense now. He was behind it all. He was testing me and I failed, but that wasn't good enough for him, was it? He went ahead and gave us the weekend from hell just because he could.'

'Get out.' Dad's voice is dangerously low, but Joe ignores him.

'Look, I'll prove it.' Joe pulls his phone from his pocket, flicking through the screens before holding it up in front of Dad. 'This is Cole Foster. He's one of your men, isn't he?' he demands. 'You didn't think of that, did you, me getting a photo of him? Because now I have proof of what you did. Your lackey didn't realise the gym takes photos of members for use on their website. You're not as clever as you think you are, are you? You've been rumbled, *mate*.'

Dad's face pales as he studies the picture, and the world stops for me. I thought it couldn't get any worse, but now the only person I thought I could trust totally in the world has betrayed me, too.

'Dad?' I ask, my mouth suddenly dry. 'Tell me it's not true.'

'He can't, can he?' Joe says triumphantly. 'Look at his face. That tells you all you need to know.'

'Show her the photo,' Dad says quietly to Joe. 'Show Beth the photo.'

Joe turns to me, holding his phone up to my face. At first, I can't quite make sense of what I'm seeing. There's a man talking to Joe, with gym equipment and people working out in the background. But as the image comes into focus, my heart starts to race.

I recognise Cole Foster.

Only I never knew him as Cole.

When I knew him, he went by another name.

Back then, he was Quinn.

My ex-boyfriend.

CHAPTER TWENTY-FOUR

Quinn

There's a saying that revenge is a dish best served cold, and I couldn't agree more – and it's especially satisfactory when it comes with a wad of cash with it.

No one died, as they also say, but yeah, harm was done. Beth is probably going to be traumatised by what happened for a while; maybe even for the rest of her life. James Winters has a big dent in his wallet and Joe's lost his meal ticket.

But you know, technically, it's not my fault. I was forced into it.

I'd never have done it if James Winters hadn't been so vindictive. When Lizzi – or Beth, as she likes to call herself now – dumped me, I was philosophical about it because I deserved it. I did the dirty on her and cheated on her, like I do with all my girlfriends. That's just who I am. I intended no malice, and it wasn't intentional and, to be honest, I never actually said we were exclusive when we got together, she just assumed. And although I told her I loved her, I say that to all the girls I get with in the heat of the moment. How was I supposed to know she'd take it so seriously? Is it really my fault she's so needy? She called me a player, amongst other things and she wasn't far wrong because I don't see myself ever settling down – commitment isn't in my nature.

So, fair enough, I thought, it was nice while it lasted, but I deserved to get dumped. It wasn't the end of the world for me – I mean; I liked the lifestyle and the fancy places we went to, but I knew I'd find my way there eventually on my own talents, with or without her.

Turns out, I underestimated how far James Winters would go to ruin me.

My job went first; not totally unexpected, but unfair. I was on track to run IT for the entire company, so firing me wasn't just petty; it was bad business. And he didn't just let me go, he made it ugly, and accused me of fiddling my expenses. For Christ's sake, who's ever completely honest about their expense reports? Ninety-five per cent of the workforce cheat on their expenses, it's what people do. Companies almost expect it.

So I was disappointed in James; we'd got on well before me and Lizzi-Beth split and now he was making it personal and using his position to get his own back on me. He knew he wouldn't get better than me, but he was prepared to let his heart rule his head over a business decision because his little girl needed to grow up and stop being such a baby.

So there I was, jobless with all my prospects at The Winters Group gone forever. Annoying and unnecessary, but not a major problem for me because I had the skills, the qualifications and the experience. I'd have to start over, work my way back up again, especially because James Winters wasn't going to give me a glowing reference, but truthfully, I wasn't worried.

Turns out I should have been. Because James Winters put the word out; employ Quinn and say goodbye to doing business with The Winters Group ever again. And since his company has its fingers in just about everything going, that effectively blacklisted me from any major company. The only job I could get was working for a little startup that had never heard of James Winters or The Winters Group. The hours were long, the pay low and the owner a complete arsehole. I could have stuck it out but I quickly realised that there was no prospect of any advancement because the business wasn't going anywhere. It was already struggling when I hopped on board and all the signs were that it would be folding within the year.

Which is exactly what happened; in less than

nine months I was jobless again.

Is that why I did it?

Partly. There was the money, of course, but I also wanted revenge. Mostly on James, for what he did to me, but also on Lizzi-Beth, or whatever she's calling herself these days. She needed a little reality check to knock her off that high horse of self-righteousness. When we were together, she never shut up about how people judged her on her looks, on her dad's money, and how no one saw her *true worth*.

Blah, blah, blah.

Get over yourself, I used to think, as she whined on as if she had something to actually moan about.

Entitled. Spoilt. Deluded. A total princess.

Those words describe her exactly and a dose of harsh reality for a weekend wouldn't kill her and might actually make her appreciate what she had instead of whinging about it. She was never in any *real* danger, but it wouldn't hurt her to think she was.

As for Joe, he's a total prick, another one who thought life owed him something. He constantly boasted about making it out of his tough background as if that made him special, but the second he saw an easy meal ticket, he latched on and hung on for dear life. He played innocent, telling me he didn't know Lizzi-Beth was rich when they met, but I'm not stupid; I can spot a liar a mile away.

Because it takes one to know one.

Befriending him was embarrassingly easy and telling him I was a counsellor was a stroke of genius, because he thought that made me some sort of priest who could hear his confession. Telling him that was a spur-of-the-moment decision; we were chatting, and I just dropped it in there to see his reaction and he picked up on it immediately. I knew then that I had him on the hook. All I had to do was bide my time and wait for the right moment to offer to help him relieve James Winters of two million pounds.

It didn't take a lot to convince him I had the perfect solution to his problems. A weekend away in the country, a pile of cash, and the perfect opportunity to make James Winters look like a gullible fool who'd been scammed by someone smarter than him. Nobody would get hurt, I reassured Joe. His eyes lit up when I explained it to him and he fell for it like a charm, although the closer the weekend got, the more nervous he became. I wasn't surprised when he tried to back out but I soon closed that down by telling him that, of course, he could cancel, but he'd have to pay. His face when I told him was a picture; I so wanted to laugh and I don't quite know how I didn't. What a bloody idiot.

The weekend of the hit, I impressed myself with how smoothly it all went. The only hiccup was when Lizzi-Beth faked cutting her wrists; that wasn't in the plan. It was panic stations for a while until we realised she wasn't actually in danger at all. Clever, though, doing that, and I'll admit, I was impressed. I even thought that maybe I'd misjudged her a bit, and she wasn't such a princess after all. When she tried to escape, she went up in my estimation again because that took guts and I never thought she had any. This was a Lizzi-Beth I hadn't seen before and if she'd been a bit more like that when we were together, maybe I wouldn't have felt the need to cheat on her.

Yeah, probably not.

Anyway, her escape attempt changed little because it was all working out as it should. She took a real risk, though, running, because I wouldn't want to be caught by those scary-arse dogs.

And then it was all over for them and they were back home, safe and sound.

But I wasn't done yet.

I half wondered if Joe was going to confess to her, but he kept his mouth shut so I let a week go by, just to let him think he'd got away with it, before I started winding Lizzi-Beth up. Sending those texts was just the first step in getting her to question Joe but that was all I needed to do because she wasn't exactly loyal, was she? I had plenty more tricks ready but I never had to use them, because despite all her self-righteousness, she was quick to assume the worst about him.

Her husband. The man she'd married. That's how much she really thought of him.

Still, all's well that ends well.

And it ended very well for me because I walked away with a million and a half after paying off the muscle and bribing one of the alarm installers at Lizzi-Beth's house to fiddle around with Joe's computer for me. He didn't know what he was doing it for and I paid him enough money for him not to ask questions or blab to anyone. Hacking into Joe's computer remotely was a doddle after that.

So easy.

And as for James Winters? He won't come after me, I'm certain of that. He won't risk the humiliation, the terrible publicity, the damage to his reputation. More importantly, that kidnapping scared him. It showed him he and Lizzi-Beth are not untouchable and that no one is completely safe. He won't take the chance of me pulling something like that again.

Besides, he'd have to find me first and I've moved on, covered my tracks, started afresh. I have a new name, new background, the lot. Quinn Barrington no longer exists because, like I said, I'm talented, one of the best in the computer business.

No scrap that. I am *the* best.

James Winters could spend his life looking, and he wouldn't find me. I'm not in the UK anymore; it's not big enough for me. It's full of small-minded people with insignificant lives and narrow-minded ideas, so I've moved somewhere far away, somewhere much bigger. More opportunities, more scope, more cities to get lost in.

Win some, lose some, as they say.
And I always win.

CHAPTER TWENTY-FIVE

Three months later

I have a new job now, a permanent position in a large accountancy firm. I'm gradually settling in, finding my feet, making new friends. My leg and ankle are completely healed and back to normal. It's as if they were never broken.

Unlike my heart.

When it all gets too much for me and the memories of that weekend and the weeks afterwards come flooding back to me, I remind myself that it's early days.

Time heals. I hope.

Joe and I aren't together, but he's trying his best to make amends. He says he refuses to give up on us. He still comes to the house and while at first I refused to let him in, I eventually relented because we're adults, not children who can never speak to each other again.

In the beginning, there was a lot of anger to work through. I did most of the shouting and blaming, and Joe sat there and took it. Then we started talking – really talking, more than we ever did before. Joe opened up about his childhood and told me the harsh unvarnished truth, and that was an eye opener for me because although he'd told me it was hard, he'd never told me just how bad it really was. He wasn't after sympathy, but it made me understand how different his life was from mine; how privileged my own upbringing had been.

He's been completely honest with me about how he felt and why he did it. He thinks maybe he went mad for a little while, that the promise of easy money was just too much temptation to cope with. He realises now that he should have talked to me about how he felt and not Quinn, or Cole, as he knew him. Whilst I thought everything was fine, Joe was struggling, and I feel guilty for not realising that. I should have been there for him and I let him down, because I was too fixated on my own feelings and how everything affected me, so I'm not entirely blameless, either.

Uncharacteristically, Dad is staying silent about Joe, telling me only that I'm the one who has to decide whether to forgive him. Finding out it was Quinn who was behind the kidnap has rocked Dad, as it did me. Neither of us knew Quinn hated us so much, or how far he was prepared to go to get his revenge. Dad even admitted that maybe he treated Quinn badly; that he was vindictive and went too far.

But that's not the reason we never contacted the police. Dad knows how good Quinn was at his job; he's convinced that the police would never find him and that if, by some miracle, they did, Quinn will have made sure that there would be no evidence to implicate him. What would be the point, Dad said, in involving the police and suffering all the resultant bad publicity, if there's no chance of catching him or if they did, of any jury convicting him?

It would be pointless. Better to put Quinn and his actions behind us.

So that's where we're at now. Me and Joe are in a kind of limbo; neither of us has made any move to start divorce proceedings and I think that's a sign that deep down, neither of us is prepared to admit that our marriage is truly over. Can we move on from this and build a new life together?

The life we always wanted?

Maybe; because despite everything, I still love him. The Joe that I first met is still here, and he hasn't changed. The Joe who never knew who I'd once been or who my father was, or how much money he had, I still love that Joe. That has to count for something, doesn't it, that Joe never married me because he thought I was rich and could give him an easy life? When we met, he wanted me for myself and nothing more. He loved me for who I was and no one other man has ever done that. If we'd lived in our own little world and he'd never learned of Dad's wealth, then none of this would have happened.

Dad's wealth turned Joe's head; sent him temporarily mad.

Who knows how I would have behaved if I'd had the same childhood as Joe? I've had it easy, so how can I ever judge him?

Nothing can change the past and what Joe did but everyone makes mistakes, don't they? One day in the not too distant future, I hope I'll be able to forgive Joe, and we can move forward and be together.

Start afresh.

Because everyone deserves a second chance, don't they?

THE END

Thank you so much for reading this book, I really do appreciate it. I do hope that you've enjoyed it and if you have, I'd be thrilled if you took the time to leave a review or star rating on Amazon/and or Goodreads.

Printed in Dunstable, United Kingdom

71221312R00161